SPACE
MERCENARIES

by
A. BERTRAM CHANDLER

PRIORY BOOKS

Published by PRIORY BOOKS
London, England

First printed by
Ace Books, Inc.

Produced in Israel for
PRIORY BOOKS, London, England

I

"I LIKE MONEY," remarked the ex-Empress Irene. "I have always liked money. But I possess a conscience. A luxury," she added thoughtfully, "which I can now afford to indulge."

"Mmph?" grunted her husband, as he made a fractional adjustment to the gain control.

"When I was Empress," she went on, "things were different. I could do, or order to be done, things that now would make me shudder. As a private citizen I can weigh the consequences—the immediate ones, I mean, not the long-range ones. It's no longer my concern what will work out best for the Empire a hundred or a thousand years from to-day. But I am concerned with the effects of any action of mine upon the ordinary people *now*."

Trafford sighed, and straightened up from the chart tank with which he had been tinkering. It was obvious to him that he would not be allowed to work undisturbed. He turned to look at his wife, to look up at his wife. He was a small man, compact and wiry, a typical naval officer of his day and age, while she, like all of those selected, through the years, to occupy the non-hereditary throne of the Empire, conformed to the standards imposed by the Committee, the so-called talent scouts. She did not need a crown to elevate her, physically, above general mankind. She was tall, but too beautifully proportioned ever to be described as big. An illusion of imperial robes hung about the plain business suit that she was wearing, and her gleaming hair, in which a single bright jewel rested, was a natural coronet.

Trafford regarded her not without appreciation, then demanded, "Just what is biting you, Irene?"

She collapsed gratefully into one of the control room chairs. "To begin with, *Captain*, you shouldn't have to ask *me*. In any properly organized merchant vessel it is the Master who goes ashore on business, while the Mate stays aboard to look after the ship."

"In the Navy," pointed out Trafford, "business is the concern of the Paymaster Commander."

"You aren't in the Navy any longer. You resigned your commission. Remember? And we don't run to a Purser in this wagon."

Trafford sighed again, then put away his tools. He went to one of the other chairs, swiveled it so that he was facing Irene when he sat down. He filled and lit his pipe, deriving a certain pleasure from the fact that it was no longer necessary for him to request permission to smoke in the Imperial Presence. To begin with, Irene was no longer Empress. Secondly, she was his wife. Finally, she was on the Articles as Mate, while he was Master—monarch (in theory) of all that he surveyed.

He said mildly, speaking through the self-generated smoke screen, "Suppose we get all this division of responsibility ironed out now, my dear. You may be the Mate—but you are also the owner. *Wanderer* is your property. Therefore, it is only right and proper that you do the dickering with the ship brokers."

"Legally speaking," she told him, "the Master has the power to sell the ship."

"But it's not legalities that have you so worried. What was all that about your conscience?"

She laughed ruefully. "Yes. That's what's worrying me. It all seemed so simple—to hand off this alleged yacht to anybody wanting a relatively cheap warship, and then to blow the proceeds on a nice, economical little star tramp. But this is the trouble, Benjamin. The only reasonable offers for the ship are from people to whom I wouldn't dream of selling so much as a peashooter. And it's so damned obvious what's behind it all. That blasted Committee has been pulling strings and dropping hints and dispensing back-handers. For example—the Empire does not, *officially*, approve of the Duchy of Waldegren, but the Waldegrenese have their uses. Just by behaving as they always have behaved—and always will behave until they're taught a lesson—they deter their neighbors, the semi-autonomous Tashkent Commonwealth, from screaming too loudly for full autonomy. As Empress I had to play along—but as a private citizen I'll see those stinking pirates in hell before I sell them my ship!"

"H'm. So that's why the Navy was never allowed to take really strong action against Waldegren and one or two other pirate nests. . . ."

"Yes, my innocent Benjamin. That's why. Of course, we had to make noises of disapproval about such things as piracy and confrontation—but we never *did* anything. And there were always ways and means of seeing that the more unsavory planetary governments never went short of arms and ships. . . ." She slumped deeper into her chair, frowning heavily. "So it looks as though our learned friend Dr. Pettigrew pushed off an urgent, top priority spacegram to his fellow Committeemen as soon as we berthed—and then, flashing his identification, demanded an audience with the Planetary Manager and dropped him a few hints. Then the P.M. did some hint dropping in his turn—to the bosses of Dolkar Hulls Incorporated, the only firm of ship brokers on this hick world. The word has been passed that the Empire will not, repeat not, be pleased if Miss Irene Smith sells her armed yacht to any buyer not approved by said Empire."

Trafford relit his pipe. He said thoughtfully, "I wasn't happy about this business from the start. Don't these people think there's something odd about a private citizen owning a vessel that's practically a light cruiser?"

"You should know, Benjamin, that they think that every damn thing about Terrans is odd. A reptile just does not have the same thought processes as a mammal. But they realize which side their bread is buttered on, make no mistake about that. They know that they, as citizens of a frontier world, are well advised to remain on friendly terms with the people on the other side of the frontier."

"But the Lady Eleanor is officially Empress now. Couldn't you persuade her to put a spoke in Pettigrew's wheel?"

"Give the wench time to recover from her brain-washing. She had a far rougher time on that hallucinogenic world than either of us. It'll be months before she's anything more than a puppet."

"So what do we do?"

"Have you any suggestions, Benjamin?"

"We could lift ship and proceed to Llinifarne. . . ."

"Only to find that a spacegram has beaten us there, and that the brokers have been warned to play ball with the Empire, or else."

"We could gut the ship of her armament and convert her into a cargo carrier."

"And who'll pay for it, Benjamin? I have, as you know, a considerable private fortune—but there wouldn't be much of it left after a conversion job. We should have no reserves whatsoever—and we shall need reserves. I know that a small, independent operator, bucking the old-established shipping lines, is licked before he starts unless he can afford a freight war. You people in the Navy don't know the first thing about ship management for profit. You're far too used to signing a requisition form and then getting everything you asked for."

"Not all the time, Irene," protested Trafford. "Some of those petty pen-pushers in the Bureau of Supply . . ."

"Somebody has to look after the taxpayer's interests." She smiled grimly. "But all this bickering is getting us nowhere. Let's just face the facts. We have on our hands a ship that's at least as good as any light cruiser in your precious Navy—and the only people willing to take her off our hands, at a fair price, are a horde of bloody-minded pirates of whom neither of us approves. We also have on our hands a bunch of highly-skilled technicians who are merely on loan to me from the Navy until such time as we sell the ship. I'm surprised that they haven't demanded that they be given passage on the same liner as Pettigrew and the prisoners. Except in times of crisis, the Navy's not used to being away from home for more than a week at a time."

"Lay off the Navy, can't you? But if it's any comfort to you, Metzenther and Bronheim are incurable bachelors. And young Tallentire is quite happy to stay with the ship as long as Susanna's here to hold his hand."

"So we can keep our Engineer, our Communications Officer, *and* the Gunnery Boy. That's good to know. Especially about the Gunnery Officer."

Trafford looked at her, trying to read her expression. She was not, he decided at last, being sarcastic. But what was she driving at?

She went on, "I wonder if your friends would be willing to do the same as you—resign their commissions?"

"We can use a first class engineer, and a trained telepath. But a gunnery specialist?"

"Just an idea . . ." she murmured. "Just an idea. But suppose you get out of that uniform which, after all, you aren't entitled to wear any longer, and dress up like a respectable shipmaster having a wander ashore, and come for a pub crawl with your Mate. . . ."

"But this chart tank . . ."

"The calibration's not all that important. Come on."

Irene was no longer Empress, but she could still give orders. *Anything for a quiet life*, thought Trafford, and went to his quarters to change.

8

II

FROM THE Terran viewpoint Slithila City had little to recommend it—but a climate congenial to reptiles is not likely to appeal to mammals. Trafford had made Slithila his first port of call after lifting from the planet of the hallucinogens, for only one reason: it was the nearest world with a regular service of interstellar passenger liners. He had wanted to get the prisoners off his hands—and Dr. Pettigrew, that overly conscientious Committeeman, out of his hair—as soon as possible. Too, according to the Directory of Port Information, Slithila City boasted a reliable firm of ship brokers. No doubt the Imperial Bureaucrats still regarded Messrs. Dolkar Hulls in that light. . . .

A cab summoned by Susanna on the ship-to-shore telephone was waiting at the airlock by the time Trafford was ready. He was pleased that Irene—who was something of a fanatic on the subject of healthy exercise—had decided not to walk. The sky was overcast, as usual, and the thin drizzle that drifted between the low spaceport buildings and the wet, gleaming hulls of the berthed ships made the day seem far colder than it actually was. The mist hung in gray, ragged curtains from the fronds of the huge tree-ferns, condensed in clammy drops that spattered down to the apron from cranes and gantries, from the overhead structures of machines that still functioned, somehow, in spite of their being overgrown with densely intertwined creepers.

A dismal, green-gray world—that was Slithila. A planet whose cities were no more than haphazard collections of low, mud-colored mounds, among which and over which flourished the ferns and the lianas. A planet with a perpetually weeping sky that was a low, dreary canopy over mile after mile of dismal swamp. A world whose natives had nonetheless contrived to become fire-making, tool-using animals and who, when the first interstellar ship from outside came in to a cautious landing, had already established colonies upon both of the planet's satellites.

The cab was the usual three-wheeled affair, with the passenger compartment air-conditioned for the comfort of the outworld customers, and with the driver's seat situated over the single rear wheel, exposed to the weather. The cabbie grinned hideously at them as they emerged from the airlock, flicked his scaly tail in the local salutation. "It iss fine day, Kapitan. Yess?"

"Fine for you, you glorified dinosaur," responded Trafford. For some obscure reason the Slithilians had been flattered by this expression, first used by an irresponsible junior officer of a visiting Earth ship and then explained, in some detail, by his embarrassed and apologetic Captain.

"To where, Kapitan?"

"Mars," answered Irene.

The driver regarded her with the expression of a petulant crocodile, then stared reproachfully at Trafford, "Kapitan, do I the orders of this egg-layer take?"

"Yes," Trafford told him, repressing a grin. "Mars, please."

They got into the vehicle. It was warm, but not too warm, in the cabin, and dry. They had an uninterrupted view in all directions from the wide windows. On some worlds such a cab would have been ideally suited to sight-seeing—but on Slithia there was little to see. The misty rain cut down visibility to less than half a mile—and, as Trafford complained, one tree fern is very like the next one, and the one before it. Traffic became heavier as they approached the city: cabs like their own, but with open passenger compartments so that the occupants could enjoy the omnipresent dampness; larger three-wheeled vehicles piled high with tarpaulin-shrouded merchandise; and a veritable army of cyclists, each peddling his tricycle with an odd, jerky motion, like a mechanical toy, each with his tail cocked in the air so that it would not foul the rear wheel.

And then there was Mars—a rectangular box of a building, its straight lines in startling contrast to the curves of the low domes surrounding it, with a mast on its roof, at the truck of which, in crimson neon, was the age-old symbol, the circle and arrowhead, for the Red Planet of Earth's solar system.

And it was strange, in this age of interstellar travel and commerce, how Mars itself still remained the symbol for aridity, for jealously hoarded water, for the climatic harshness that was the antithesis of the prevailing weather of the world of Slithila. But it was not at all strange that Mars should be a port of refuge for those Terrans exiled in the humid, muddy city—the clerical staff of shipping lines, consular officials, and the like. Inside the building the air was dry, with the acrid pungency of Martian sand, while outside it was saturated with moisture, heavy with the stink of simultaneous growth and decay. Inside there were garish reds and oranges and yellows—sand and wind-sculpted rocks, crimson lichens and the angular contortions of towering, golden cacti. Outside there was the all-pervading gray-green lushness.

Once they were through the airlock door, Irene took the lead, threading her way between the tables, at most of which there were groups of serious drinkers, to where a man was sitting alone, moodily staring at the bottle and glass before him. He looked up, then got to his feet, making a stiff little half-bow.

"Mr. Smith," said the ex-Empress, "this is my husband, Captain Trafford."

The two men shook hands, with conventional firmness, and

11

Trafford studied this new acquaintance with some curiosity. Never, he decided, had he seen such an *ordinary* looking individual. Hair-colored hair. Eye-colored eyes. Face-shaped face. And the clothing was the drab, gray cover-all that was almost a uniform for the privates of the armies of industries and commerce, although quality and cut put its wearer into at least an officer's category.

"Perhaps you will drink with me," the man said as the others seated themselves. "I can recommend the *tequila*." He pressed the call button set in the center of the table.

"Before we go any further," asked Irene sharply, "is this place bugged?"

"No," Smith told her. "Besides, I have a distorter. And it's switched on. But it's no use here. Wait."

With a soft whirring of caterpillar treads a robowaiter—modeled on the all-purpose robots employed by the first Martian colonists—scurried towards them over the dry sand covering the floor. Its receptor lenses glared at them redly. "No service," it said, flatly, mechanically. "No service. No service."

"Don't panic," Smith told it. His hand went to a side pocket. There was a barely audible click.

"No service," it reiterated. "No service. No service . . ."

Irene's hand went up to the jewel in her hair. She said, "I had intended to make a wire-recording of this conversation but . . ."

Her slim fingers made an almost imperceptible twisting motion, and the robot said, "Your orders please. Your orders please."

"Another bottle of *tequila*," said Smith. "With salt and lemon slices. And two more glasses."

"The place seems to be well anti-bugged," commented Trafford.

"Too right," agreed Smith. "The proprietor maintains that

12

there should be one place in this city where people can drink and talk like civilized human beings without having to worry about spies, industrial or . . . otherwise. Should the offending electronic gadgetry not be switched off at once, after a few seconds, the robowaiter won't just say, 'No service'. It will shout the words—and the customers who want to enjoy their drinks in peace and quiet are not slow in taking action."

"Telepaths?" asked Irene curtly.

"They're as scarce as hen's teeth. The only one that I know of is the owner himself, and should he suspect any psionic eavesdropping, it's the bum's rush for the eaves-dropper."

"Just as well we didn't bring Metzenther." The robowaiter brought the drinks. While Smith was filling the glasses Irene salted a slice of lemon, nibbled it thoughtfully, and then took a sip of the fiery spirit. "Not bad," she commented.

"No, it's not. I think that the Martian *tequila* is even better than the so-called genuine stuff from Mexico."

"Is it?" Her manner became businesslike. "Now, Mr. Smith, you gave me to understand, when we had our brief talk in the office of Dolkar Hulls, that you had a proposition that would interest me."

"I have. You, of all people, know that it will be almost impossible to sell your yacht to a buyer of whom *you* approve."

"What do you mean—*me*, of all people?"

The man laughed softly. "I don't know what's been going on—but I do know that a very pale and subdued Empress Irene has booked passage aboard the Trans-Galactic Clipper *Lightning*, and that she is accompanied by her personal physician and adviser, one Dr. Pettigrew. And I know that this same Dr. Pettigrew is a ranking member of the famous Selection Committee, and also that he has been breathing hard down the neck of the Planetary Manager. . . ."

"I also know, Miss Smith—if I may call you by the name under which you are registered as the owner of *Wanderer*—that although an occasional member of our clan can afford a space-going yacht, nobody, except yourself, owns a yacht that is a tarted-up version of an Imperial Navy light cruiser. So, Your Imperial Highness . . ."

"Irene Smith was my maiden name," she told him coldly. "I am now Mrs. Trafford. I am the legal owner of the armed yacht *Wanderer*. Now, what is your proposition?"

"You no longer have any connection with the Imperial Government?"

"No more than any other private citizen of the Empire. I can assure you of that. So, talk. The hints that you dropped earlier today interested me. See if you can interest Captain Trafford."

"I will try," said Smith quietly. "To begin with, I am employed by Dolkar Hulls as their Terran Adviser. In this capacity I advised against arranging the sale of your ship to the Duchy of Waldegren. I was told by my principals that it was none of their concern if Terrans wished to slaughter each other as long as they, Dolkar Hulls, received a commission on the deal. I was told, too, that the prospective sale had been approved both by the Planetary Manager and by the representative of your Imperial Government. I have reasons for not liking the Waldegrenese, so I was pleased when Mrs. Trafford refused to sell.

"But I am not meeting you here as the representative of Dolkar Hulls."

"Then whom do you represent?" asked Irene quietly.

"GLASS."

GLASS . . . thought Trafford. Yes, it all added up. What was their slogan? "Our motives are transparently clear." And their detractors sneered, "They're too dirty to see through."

GLASS. The Galactic League for the Abolition of Suppression and Slavery.

"Aren't you getting ambitious?" queried Irene. "I thought that lending a financial helping hand to the odd revolution was as far as you ever went. But chartering a warship . . ."

"We can afford it."

"I'm pleased to hear that. I was afraid that you'd be wanting our services for free."

"We prefer to pay. After all, history tells us that mercenaries in general have a very good record of loyalty to their paymasters."

"And what do *you* say, Benjamin?" Irene seemed to be enjoying herself. "What do you say, ex-Commander Trafford, late of the Imperial Navy? Do you want to be a mercenary? Do you want to enlist under the banner of this bunch of traitors, subversives, and screwballs?"

"If they are, as they claim, on the side of the angels . . ." said Trafford dubiously.

"But they are, they are. Unfortunately their activities often run counter to Imperial Policy. But that's not *my* worry."

Trafford was silent. The conditioning of years of training was hard to shake off. As a naval officer he had always been an instrument of Imperial Policy, had always believed that the object of this policy was the greatest good for the greatest number. He met his wife's questioning stare, and then stated this belief.

"Is it?" she countered. "Is it?" She laughed. "I know too much. I allowed myself to be kidded along when I was Empress, the glamorous figurehead who was, actually, quite a lot more than a figurehead. But that experience on the hallucinogenic planet opened my eyes. Frankly, I want to do something to make up for the many *wrong* things—and to hell with the Empire's long-term policy!—that I did when I was Empress. No, not for nothing. I know that do-gooders are responsible for more harm than good, and are justly despised by the people with whose lives they tamper. But—how does that quotation go?—*I don't mind making a stab at saving the sum of things for pay.*

"Spoken like a true mercenary," said Smith.

Trafford said to him bluntly, "You want a warship. So you think that there will be fighting."

"What else is a warship for?"

"Sometimes just for show. But if there is fighting, I'll not turn my guns on any vessel of the Imperial Navy."

"We shall respect your loyalties, Captain Trafford. But we have yet to discover whether or not you will be loyal to *us*. You and your officers will be handled very cautiously indeed, until we are sure of you. But this opportunity of obtaining the services of a cruiser was far too good to let it slip by."

"I shall need my specialists," Trafford said to Irene. "But will they be willing to work for an organization like GLASS?"

"I think they will. Like us, they were able to stand well back, to take a good look at themselves, their loyalties and their beliefs and their prejudices."

"Tallentire missed out on the deal, and so did Susanna."

"Susanna is loyal to me, and Tallentire will go where she goes."

"I'm still not sure about it all . . ." murmured Trafford.

"It's employment," Irene told him cheerfully. "And the pay's good." She looked at Smith. "Is it?" she asked.

"We've yet to draw up the contract," the man told her. "But we are not without funds." He smiled. "We have been known to accept contributions from the people we help."

"So you're mercenaries yourselves," said Irene.

"I suppose we are. But ethical ones. And I hope that you will be able to say the same about yourselves."

III

So THEY WERE mercenaries, all of them.

The specialist officers had agreed to stay in the ship out of personal loyalty to Trafford and to Irene—and after all, Tallentire said, their commissions had been signed by her and not by the present Empress. She thought it wisest not to enlighten the officers on this point. And then Irene, more or less disguised by dark glasses, a wide-brimmed hat, and a high-collared coat, had stormed aboard *Lightning* a bare half hour prior to lifting. She had sought out Pettigrew and bullied him into letting her see the woman who had been her stand-in, the Lady Eleanor—and who was now, officially, the Empress Irene. She had persuaded her to append her signature to the documents releasing Metzenther, Bronheim, and Tallentire from the Imperial Naval Service. She had watched the liner's Captain and Chief Officer, stiff and formal in the presence of Royalty, witness the scrawled *Irene Imperatrix*. It was not the first time that Eleanor had written those words. As stand-in she had often signed official papers and, in fact, by this time would have found it hard to put anything down in her own handwriting.

And then Irene, taking Trafford by the hand, had led him gently but firmly through the jungles of red tape by which merchant shipping is overgrown. To begin with, the Terran Consul had to issue provisional Certificates of Competency to Trafford and the others, their Naval commissions being regarded as proof that they were adequately qualified. (Irene, as she sourly reminded her husband, had been obliged to gain *her* Master Astronaut's Certificate the hard way.) Then the Consul General put Trafford's name on the Register as Master.

Next, Trafford had to open *Wanderer*'s Articles of Agreement at the Shipping Office. This task completed, he stood by while the others signed in their various capacities—Irene as Mate, Tallentire as Second Mate, Bronheim as Chief Engineer, Metzenther as Communications Officer, and Susanna as Purser.

Finally, when they were all seated around a table in Mars, he protested, "But *Wanderer* is *not* a merchant vessel."

"In the eyes of the Law she is," Irene told him. "She's privately owned. She wears the flag of no Navy. . . ."

"But a merchant vessel with laser projectors and guided missiles!" went on Trafford.

"Just a defensive armament," she said airily. "Quite legal. After all, I got *my* gunnery training in the defensively armed ships of the Dog Star Line."

Tallentire muttered something about an armed rabble and she snapped, "Pipe down, Second Mate!"

The Gunnery Officer sat back in his chair, his lean, darkly handsome face sulky. *He takes himself too seriously,* Trafford thought. And then he looked at Susanna, who, in appearance, could almost have been the young man's sister. She was regarding Tallentire with a quizzical expression. She caught his eye and smiled slightly, and he flashed her a white grin in return. The Captain, watching the brief interchange, was relieved. Susanna would be able to keep Tallentire in order.

"But just when does defense end and attack start?" asked Trafford.

"That," answered Irene, "has been a fruitful field for legal quibbling ever since there was a line of demarkation drawn between the merchant ship and the fighting ship. This much is clear—the Master of a merchantman is entitled to resist seizure or destruction by force of arms. But as to whether or not he is entitled to fire the first shot . . ." She shrugged.

"I'm the Captain of this wagon," went on Trafford. "Or,

if you insist that everything has to be strictly Merchant Service, the Master. I still don't know what I'm supposed to be doing, or what I *can* do. These GLASS people have chartered us—and they want us for our armament rather than for our very limited cargo capacity. Wouldn't it be simpler all round if we were classed as a privateer?"

"It would be," agreed his wife. "It would be. But we're still under Terran registry and, frankly, I just can't see what used to be *my* government issuing Letters of Marque to a ship which, firstly, is owned by myself and which, secondly, is on charter to a barely legal and definitely subservice organization. So we shall have to be careful, Benjamin. Very, very careful. Opening fire at the wrong time on the wrong people could well lead to our being declared pirates—and we already know what that entails."

"May I join you?" It was Smith, a bulging briefcase under his arm. With his free hand he pulled a chair up to the table, maneuvered it into the space made for him by Bronheim and Metzenther. He opened the case, took from it various papers. He said, "I've been in trouble with my principals—my GLASS superiors, that is, not the management of Dolkar Hulls. They thought that I had been in too great a hurry to snap you up and were completely at a loss as to what to do with you. But we have found employment for you at last.

"You know, of course, that the main export from this world is various antibiotic drugs. We have such a shipment for Antrim. You know the planet?"

"I know of it," said Irene. "One of the Lost Colonies, out in the Cepheus Sector. Settled by the survivors of *Lode Antrim*. Within the boundaries of the Hallichek Hegemony, but autonomous."

"I must admit," Smith told her, "that our Imperial authorities keep themselves remarkably well informed."

"Take it from me, they don't. All that information I picked up when I was in the Dog Star Lines. We had an engineer who originally came from Antrim."

"Cargo . . ." muttered Tallentire disgustedly.

"But important cargo, sir," said Smith. "Antrim is in a bad way. The Hallicheki have resented for quite a while this outpost of human culture well within their boundaries. For various reasons, which I am sure that Mrs. Trafford will appreciate, they do not wish to declare war upon Antrim—but there are other ways of bringing pressure to bear. A blockade, for instance. Their blockade is no more than the exercise of the right to detain and search all shipping navigating their territorial Space. Insofar as the urgently needed biotics are concerned, it is claimed that they are prohibited imports into the Hegemony. After all, most of them are, insofar as the Hallicheki are concerned, violent and habit-forming intoxicants.

"Be that as it may, they are needed on Antrim, sorely needed. There is the outbreak of a new pulmonary disease—it hasn't been named yet—that already has almost reached plague proportions."

"Blockade running . . ." said Tallentire hopefully.

"Not quite as good as piracy, dear, but it will have to do," said Susanna.

"What do you say?" Trafford asked his wife. "After all, *you* are the owner."

"Damned buck-passer!" she growled. "But we're being paid by these people, so we have to deliver the goods."

IV

THE LOADING did not take long; even though *Wanderer* was not designed for the carriage of cargo, as a warship, she was equipped for the rapid handling of essential stores. All that the Slithilan stevedores had to do was to place the crates onto a platform, from which the ship's own system of conveyor belts swiftly carried them to the storerooms, where other handling machinery stacked them securely. Refueling and provisioning occupied almost no time at all; hydroponics tanks and the yeast, tissue, and algae vats required no replenishment, and all that was taken aboard was a small supply of local delicacies that would afford variety—swamp lizard steaks, umbrella fern fronds and the like. And a single ingot of uranium would supply power enough to drive them clear across the Galaxy.

And then Smith, having drunk to the success of the voyage in the wardroom, was saying his good-byes. "I'll not presume to teach you your own business, Captain," he said to Trafford. "But be careful. A blockade runner is breaking no laws except those of the power that has imposed the blockade—unless she shows her teeth, uses her teeth . . ."

"Do you want this cargo to go through, or don't you?" Irene asked him bluntly.

"Of course, Mrs. Trafford. But . . ."

"But you don't want *us* to get *you* into trouble with the Imperial Government. I suppose that you have a concealed recorder somewhere on your person, so that your final admonition can be played back, if necessary, as evidence that you enjoined us to stay strictly this side of legality."

"And you wanted a ship with armament," pointed out Tallentire. "Didn't you, now?"

Smith grinned. "All right, all right. There was no harm in trying to keep my own yardarm clear, was there? So—we, of GLASS, want this shipment to go through. Speaking for myself, I'm not very fussy as to how you get it through—but, still speaking for myself, I should not like to see you people on trial for piracy. If the ship is merely seized, of course, and condemned as a prize, then GLASS will pay the agreed upon indemnity to her owner—*unless she has committed any grossly illegal act before her seizure.* Understood?"

"Understood," replied Irene curtly. She added, "As for the piracy angle—the penalty for that crime is to be pushed out through the airlock without a spacesuit. That's a remarkably unpleasant end that none of us wishes to risk."

"As I said," commented Smith, "you people know your own business. Anyway, happy landings to you all." He shook hands with *Wanderer's* crew and then was escorted by Susanna to the airlock.

It was lifting stations then, and Trafford, while still waiting for the Port Controller's clearance, saw Smith, relatively tall and straight, standing in the middle of a group of kangaroo-like Slithilans, his hand raised in salute. The sibilant voice of the Controller whispered from the speaker of the transceiver to wish them *bon voyage,* and with the sudden cessation of the warning bells came the odd sensation of lightness that told that the Inertial Drive was in operation, the sensation of lightness that was immediately transformed to one of heaviness once the ship's landing gear was clear of the apron.

They ballooned through the drizzle, through the low overcast, slowly at first, then with increasing speed. They soared through the last tenuous shreds of cloud and then Slithila was below them, a vast plain of dazzling white vapor, a plain that suddenly became the surface of a sphere. Above them, around them, was the familiar black space with its shimmering drifts of distant suns.

Slowly, to the whine of her gyroscopes, *Wanderer* turned about her short axis, while Irene identified the target star and Trafford carefully centered the point of radiance in the cartwheel sight.

On the console the pilot lights of the Mannschenn Drive glowed amber. Trafford punched the *Start* button. At once the almost supersonic keening of the ever-precessing rotors was a disturbing background to every other noise in the ship. Outside the ports the universe went mad, and every star became a distorted spiral of pulsing, multi-colored light. *Wanderer* was on her way, driven ahead in three-dimensional space by her Inertial Drive but making, in effect, stern way in that other dimension of the continuum, drifting backwards in time. The voyage would not be instantaneous—but it would be as nearly so as Bronheim, who had been one of the Imperial Navy's acknowledged Interstellar Drive experts, could make it.

It was seven years from Slithila to Antrim at the speed of light. It took seven weeks for *Wanderer* to get within half a light year of the Antrim sun—a voyage that, *in theory,* could be accomplished in seven seconds.

Seven weeks—with Bronheim sleeping (when he did sleep) on a bunk that had been set up in the Interstellar Drive Room, with Metzenther maintaining a continual listening watch (he was lucky; he could do this asleep as well as awake) for the thoughts of other entities who might be in the neighborhood, for the Hallicheki were beings among whom telepathy, and controlled telepathy at that, was not unknown. Tallentire, spelled by Susanna, manned the Carlotti Beacon, that device used both for FTL navigation and for punching radio signals across light years almost instantaneously.

As for Irene and Trafford, they rarely left the Control Room, and they worried. Both of them had experienced war in space prior to their disastrous chase of the piratical Captain Jones—but it had not been in these conditions. Both of them—Irene as an officer of an armed merchantman and Trafford as a warship captain—had fought sometimes, had run sometimes, had often done both. This time, if the legalities were to be observed, they could only run.

"It's all that we can do, Benjamin, if we're challenged," complained Irene. "Even if it's only by an armed lighter. The Empire is on friendly terms with the Hegemony. The attitude is that if the Antrimmers *will* set up house in the middle of a hen-roost, they must expect to get pecked."

"It wasn't their fault that they were cast away there," said Trafford. "The Ehrenhaft Drive was a chancy affair at the best, and it's a miracle that any of the old gauss-jammers ever fetched up where they were supposed to."

"Yes, yes, I know all that. I also know that the Empire offered, some years ago, to transport them all from their precious planet to a suitable world within *our* borders. They turned the offer down. Perhaps they're not to be blamed. That engineer I was telling friend Smith about, the one who was with me in the old *Schnauzer* . . . Connolly was his name. He used to hit the turps now and again and get dreadfully homesick, and babble about green mountains sloping down to the sea, and fluffy white clouds lazily sailing across a soft blue sky, and the smell of peat smoke fragrant in the dusk. How did he put it? An Emerald Isle in the black ocean of space. . . . And now the Hallicheki—and *they* hadn't even gotten as far as interplanetary flight when *Lode Antrim* wandered into their neck of the woods, let alone interstellar—want that world for themselves. I can't say that I blame them. It's far, far better than some of the dumps that they've already colonized, with a reasonably dense atmosphere just made to order for avians. So they're exerting pressure on the Antrimmers, hoping that they'll tell the Empire that they've changed their minds about being relocated."

"But the Antrimmers have a legal right to their planet," argued Trafford. "Every civilized race agrees on the principles of Space Law, and one of them is that the mere planting of a flag on a hitherto undiscovered world doesn't constitute a valid claim, whereas the establishment of a self-sustaining colony does."

"Agreed. But we have to admit that the Hallicheki have the legal right to detain and search vessels navigating their territorial space, and to seize any cargo that has been declared contraband by the Hegemony."

"We should have signed on a lawyer before we lifted from Slithila," said Trafford disgustedly.

"But you, as the Master, *are* a lawyer of sorts. Of course, if you had a *real* Certificate of Competency you would have passed an examination in, among all the other things, Space Law. Luckily that bastard Jones didn't dump my books while he was cavorting around in my ship. They're all still in the bookcase. I suggest that you start studying."

Susanna, who had been listening to the conversation with interest, hastily transferred her attention to the Carlotti Beacon. Her slim fingers played over the keyboard, the intricately convoluted antenna swiveled on its mount, hunting, hunting. . . . A wriggling worm of green luminosity came alive behind the face of the oscilloscope.

"Company . . ." muttered the girl. "We have company. And close."

"Make it action stations!" snapped Irene to Trafford, but he had already punched the button.

V

IN A MATTER of seconds all hands were in the Control Room: Tallentire, who went straight to the Gunnery Console with the speed and the grace of a lean, hunting cat, a cat with claws; Bronheim, bulky and stolid, walking to the remote engine controls with a deliberation that was not as slow as it looked; the tall, gangling, gleaming-domed Metzenther, wearing a dressing gown instead of a uniform, a plain, dark robe that should have been decorated with cabalistic symbols.

"Keep your paws off those firing studs, Mr. Tallentire!" ordered Trafford sharply.

"I haven't got a target yet, sir," the Gunnery Officer pointed out.

"Just don't get trigger-happy, that's all. Mr. Bronheim, whoever it is that Susanna has picked up may attempt temporal synchronization . . ."

"I'm ready for them," growled the engineer.

"Mr. Metzenther, we're picking up signals on the Carlotti equipment. Have *you* heard anything?"

"I . . . I was dreaming when the Alarm sounded. . . ."

Irene was about to make angry comment when Trafford stopped her with an upraised hand. He was far more experienced than she in dealing with the psionic communications experts, the so-called commissioned crystal-gazers. He knew something of their powers—and their limitations. He knew that a vocalized thought could be picked up as a signal *en clair*, provided that the vocalization was in a language with which the telepath was familiar. But with vocalization in a strange language, or thoughts with no vocalization whatsoever . . .

"What were you dreaming?" he asked.

"I was a bird, one of a large number of birds. Hawks they were, or something like hawks. And there below us was another bird—a fat, unsuspecting pigeon . . ."

"Not so unsuspecting . . ." Trafford murmured. "Susanna, try to get a fix on those people—or hawks. And you, Mr. Metzenther, just relax. Any more stray thoughts that drift into your head, just let us know."

"The hawks are still there," muttered the telepath. "They will swoop soon. . . ."

"Let them," remarked Tallentire happily. "We're no pigeon!"

"But we are, Mr. Tallentire. We are. But with a good turn of speed and enough intelligence to carry out evasive tactics . . ."

"A trace on the Mass Proximity Indicator," announced Irene. "More than one ship, I think. Could be a squadron."

"They are still trying to synchronize," reported Bronheim. "But they aren't being very clever about it."

"Let them try." Trafford turned to Irene. "But I don't think that it will do any harm to establish ship-to-ship contact on the Carlotti equipment. The fact that we first picked them up on it indicated that they must have similar gear themselves."

"Yes. It will give us some idea of what we're up against. Susanna!"

"Ma'am?"

"See if you can get any joy out of that transistorized Mobius strip."

The girl, a frown of concentration on her thin face, worked tensely at the controls. Suddenly a squawking, clucking torrent of sound burst from the speaker. Susanna waited for a lull, then spoke into the microphone in a clear, cool voice.

"Interstellar ship *Wanderer* calling unidentified squadron. *Wanderer* calling unidentified squadron. Come in, please."

There was another spate of clucking and squawking, and then a single voice speaking in English. It reminded Trafford of the ancient parrot that had been a wardroom pet in one of the ships in which he had served.

"*Vanderer*," it said. "*Vanderer*. Hear this, *Vanderer*. Ve are the Hallicheki. Ve are the Seventh Cruiser Squadron. Vhere from, *Vanderer*? Vhere to?"

"Tell them," ordered Irene.

"*Wanderer*, from Slithila to Antrim."

"Vhat is your cargo?"

"Tell them," Irene ordered again.

"Antibiotics."

"Heave to, *Vanderer*, for boarding and search."

"I'll take over," said Irene. She got up from her chair, went to stand by the Carlotti Beacon equipment. She took the microphone that Susanna handed to her. "I am sorry," she stated flatly. "But that is impossible."

"Heave to. Heave to. That is an order."

"We can't. The governor of our Drive is playing up. Until it has been adjusted, we shall not be able to maintain temporal synchronization with you."

"*Vanderer*, shut down your Drive. Ve vill send engineers to help you to make repairs."

Irene looked appealingly at Bronheim, who whispered, "Tell them we can't shut down. If we do, after a long period of operation in a fluctuating temporal precession field, we shall lose all the mercury in the main ballistic."

"Should we?" she whispered back, her hand over the microphone.

The engineer grinned. "Well, we *could*. . . ."

"All right." She took her hand away from the instrument, passed on what Bronheim had said.

"Ve have *tons* of mercury in our stores," came the reply.

"Not Mercury 196," murmured Bronheim. "Say that the Mark XVII Mannschenn Drive Unit *must* use only 196. . . ."

"I'll take your word for it." Then, into the microphone, "Our Drive is a new, experimental model. It will function only if one of the rarer isotopes of mercury is used in the ballistic." She added hopefully, "I don't suppose that you have any pure 196 in your stores . . . ?"

There was clutching and squawking as the Hallichek linguist consulted with his ship's technicians. "No. Ve do not pamper our machines. Ve have no fancy isotopes. *Vanderer!* Shut down your Drive. Shut down your Drive. Ve vill send to you mechanics to install vun of our own Units."

"Very generous," commented Irene. "But if they intend to seize the ship, they can afford it." She looked again towards Bronheim, but the engineer could do no more than make a despairing shrug. Irene answered in kind, then said to the Hallichek interpreter, "I'm sorry. We can't allow that. There is a guarantee on the Mark XVII model, and if we allow any work to be done on it by unauthorized personnel, we shan't be able to get it replaced free of charge."

"But *ve* are replacing it!"

"Not with another Mark XVII, you aren't."

"They are annoyed with us," contributed Metzenther. "I am picking up the impression of a mob of frenzied hens milling around a barnyard. . . ."

"Shut down the Drive!" squawked the speaker. "Shut down your Drive!"

"Mr. Metzenther," said Irene to the telepath, "do you get any impression of immediate action of any kind?"

"No, ma'am. That image of barnyard fowls in a tizzy still persists. And there's another image—that of a fat, juicy worm vanishing down its hole before the beak closes on it

. . . and the picture of another beak, open, waiting at the other end of the hole."

"Of course. Prize money is prize money, and they just hate to think that it will go to the crews of the ships maintaining the blockade in close orbit about Antrim."

"But we have to return to normal Space-Time before we can come in to a landing," pointed out Trafford.

"We do. We do—but where?"

"Four hundred miles outside the Exosphere is usually considered safe enough, although it could be rather too close to the inner Van Allen Belt for comfort. . . ."

"And our bird-brained friends will have plenty of time to pounce before we get down to the surface. But they *are* bird-brained—the impressions that Metzenther has picked up are proof enough of that. I think that we shall be able to deliver the goods—the laws of both physics and psychology are on our side!"

VI

Wanderer could have outrun the Hallichek squadron with
ease, but she would have gained nothing by it. The warships in orbit around Antrim must have already known of
her impending arrival off the planet, even though it was quite
possible that they had not been alerted by the officer in
command of the Deep Space Patrol. Trafford had once
served in a blockading vessel and remembered, all too well,
the continuous listening watch on all the Carlotti frequencies,
the ceaseless humming of the recorders, the staffs of linguists
on instant call, the long vigil over the screens of the Mass
Proximity Indicators. Yes, it was obvious that the orbiting
ships would be expecting a Terran vessel with a cargo of
contraband, a rich prize, to appear shortly on their screens,
then to emerge into the normal continuum within range of
their missiles and projectors.

So, with the controls of the Mannschenn Drive set for
random temporal precession—but with the Inertial Drive not
operating at anything like its full capacity—the *Wanderer*
ran, and all around her, ominous sparks in the screen of the
Mass Proximity Indicator but otherwise unseeable, were the
ships of the Seventh Cruiser Squadron, still hoping to snatch
this fat prey from the very claws of the Orbital Blockade.

There was little now to be done—until the showdown. A
listening watch was maintained, and every now and again
Wanderer's people were amused by the Hallicheki's crude
attempts at psychological warfare. "Surrender to us," the
Carlotti speaker would squawk, "vhile you have time. Ve
shall be merciful; the Orbital Blockade vill not. Flight Marshal Phrymicki is a buzzard. She vill peck the flesh from your
bones. . . ." And now and again a fainter voice would break

31

in, "Do not listen to those vultures. They lie." Finally there was a fainter voice still—"Port Donegal to *Wanderer* . . . Port Donegal to *Wanderer* . . . It was a good try, and thank you. But you'd better turn back."

"Expect us when you see us, Port Donegal," was Irene's reply to this.

In the privacy of their own quarters, Trafford said, "Just what do you have in mind? I know that we should have a fair chance of fighting our way through, but I've been over all your books on Space Law and can't find any loophole through which we could fire as much as a peashooter. Once we open up, even in defense, we're classed as pirates. . . ."

She smiled smugly, "I was hoping, Benjamin, that you'd be able to work out for yourself what I have in mind. But, insofar as this sort of business is concerned, you have so much to unlearn, my dear. Your training has conditioned you for only two courses of action—to make towards inferior or equal or slightly superior forces and to run from overwhelmingly superior forces, and in either case every possible weapon will be brought to bear. But—apart from the running like hell—this situation calls for a different technique."

"We aren't even running like hell. Just what are we supposed to be doing? I'm just the Captain; nobody ever tells me anything."

"Our main weapon," she told him, "is psychology."

"Psychology?"

"Yes. As you should know, every intelligent life form in the universe has inherited the behavior pattern of its remote ancestors. One thing that we all have in common is curiosity, but outside that there is a wide range of difference. Well, you've listened to Metzenthers' version of what our fine, feathered friends are thinking and feeling. You've heard the Hallicheki squabbling over the prize—ourselves. Doesn't it all remind you of something?"

"H'm . . . Yes . . . Birds bickering over a juicy worm . . . ?"

"Precisely. Now, the Hallicheki aren't actually at war with anybody. The situation is merely one of confrontation. Legally speaking it's not even that. It could be argued that all these ships are engaged only in the enforcement of customs regulations.

"It was quite by chance that the Seventh Cruiser Squadron stumbled across us. But their Flight Marshal's an opportunist, and welcomed the opportunity for making a nice dollop of prize money. Meanwhile, the Flight Marshal of the Orbital Blockade maintains that the prize money should be hers. So there will be considerable jockeying for position around the point at which we should be re-entering the normal continuum. In all probability, all the vessels of the Orbital Blockade will be stationed there in readiness, leaving the far side of Antrim unguarded."

"Yes. I see that. But how do we get there?"

"Elementary physics, Benjamin. Very elementary. Mind you, I wouldn't dare to try it unless I had Bronheim, or somebody equally good, on the Drive controls."

"I wish you wouldn't talk in riddles," complained Trafford.

"And *I* wish that you'd get rid of the notion that all ship handling must be strictly in accordance with the Imperial Navy drill book. But see if you can work this one out, starting from an old, old axiom. *Two solid bodies cannot occupy the same space at the same time.*"

"It could be twisted . . ." murmured Trafford at last.

"It will be twisted—and we shall twist it."

VII

Trafford had always fancied himself as a navigator, but, even with the help of the ship's excellent computer, he could never have made the highly complex calculations required in the short time remaining. There were so many factors to be evaluated and balanced—the period of Antrim's orbit about its primary, and the vast, sweeping orbit of the Antrim sun about the galactic center, and galactic drift and expansion themselves.

As Irene and Bronheim, working together, fed problem after problem into the clicking machine, he could not help feeling out of things, ignored. He said nothing, but his wife, taking a brief spell from the high pressure work, read the expression on his face and told him, "But you're the Captain. You're in over-all command. You have to stay up here, in Control, just in case our feathered friends do manage to synchronize. . . ." She gave Tallentire a dirty look. "After all, we can't have the Master doing the Second Mate's work."

"I'm a gunnery specialist, ma'am," said the officer stiffly.

"You signed on as Second Mate," she told him, then laughed. "All right, I was just kidding. But in the Merchant Service we're jacks-of-all-trades." She stubbed out her cigarette in the saucer of her coffee cup, said to Trafford, "If you want Mr. Bronheim or myself, we shall be in the Computer Room. As usual."

When she was gone, Tallentire looked enquiringly at Trafford. He said, "I'm beginning to regret that I did specialize so narrowly, sir. Would you mind telling me just what *is* cooking?"

Trafford sat well back in his chair, made a business of

filling and lighting his pipe. "To begin with," he remarked, "I take it that you are familiar with the workings of the Mannschenn Drive."

"Of course," replied Tallentire indignantly. "Gyroscopic precession, and a precession at right angles to the three dimensions of space; but, nevertheless, precession within the space-time continuum."

"Near enough. Well, as the Empr . . . As my wife pointed out to me, two solid bodies cannot occupy the same space at the same time. We, of course, are one of the solid bodies. Antrim is the other one."

"H'm. I think I see what you're driving at." His manner became enthusiastic. "This, sir, could be classed as a blinding glimpse of the obvious. I see it all now. Temporally speaking, we shall be out of phase with Antrim. We shall go right through the planet as though it were nonexistent, to reemerge into the normal continuum on the other side, the side where the Orbital Blockade will not be waiting for us. It's so simple that it's amazing that nobody has ever tried it before."

"Firstly," Trafford told him sourly, "it's far from simple. Secondly, it has been tried before. We'll deal with the second point first. You may, just possibly, have heard of a pirate who called himself Black Bart. In many respects he was a military genius, and one of his contributions to the art of spatial warfare was the synchronizer. Until the principles of random precession were worked out, it was a deadly weapon. He would pick up and hunt down his victim by use of his Mass Proximity Indicator, synchronize temporal precession rates and loose off his broadside, simultaneously desynchronizing just in case the other ship replied in kind. Then he'd synchronize again, if necessary, to repeat the process. Otherwise he'd shut down his Drive and board and loot.

"Well, the Navy's backroom boys finally succeeded in duplicating this device and it was fitted to two squadrons, one of which was chasing Black Bart and the other of which was blockading his base, a planet that was nothing less than a fortress world, with projectors that had an effective range of over a thousand miles. Black Bart had only one ship, and he was outclassed and outnumbered, so he ran for home. But the squadron had him boxed in, and there was that other squadron waiting for him.

"He went on running—what else could he do?—and went on running, past the point at which any sane commander would have shut down his interstellar drive. And then, suddenly, when he was well inside the atmosphere but still going like a bat out of hell, there was an atomic explosion that devastated all of five thousand square miles of the planet's surface. *And, at the same time, one of the armored satellites, a space fortress that had been engaged in a missile duel with the blockading cruisers, ceased to exist.*

"That was the end of Black Bart. Of course, nobody knows what actually *did* happen, but the scientists came up with quite a tenable hypothesis. Black Bart, they said, tried to do what we shall be trying to do. But he didn't allow for all the factors when he made his calculations. That orbital fortress just happened to get into his way at some time prior to the actual occurrence. How shall I put it? Black Bart's *present* trajectory neatly intersected the fortress's *past* trajectory, but as his Mannschenn Drive was in operation there was temporal synchronization. And two solid bodies just cannot occupy the same space at the same time.

"So, you see, it's not so simple. And Antrim has its fair share of satellites—observatories, laboratories, relay stations, weather control stations and the like—in a wide variety of orbits. It's hard enough, at times, to make due allowance for all the ironmongery in orbit around a world when you're navigating in only three dimensions—but when you're working in four. . . ."

"I see," said Tallentire. "Or, rather, I think I see," he admitted. "And I had heard of Black Bart, but all that it says about his finish in the official histories is that he collided with one of his own orbital forts."

"Which is true enough. As a matter of fact, I didn't know the full story myself until my wife told me. When she was Empress, she used to enjoy browsing through the old naval records—the ones not accessible to the likes of us." He grinned. "Just as well that she did browse, while she had the chance."

"We hope," said Tallentire.

"We hope," agreed Trafford.

The Carlotti speaker, which had been silent for a long time, suddenly squawked, *"Vanderer! Calling Vanderer."*

Tallentire looked enquiringly at Trafford, who nodded. "I hear you," said the Gunnery Officer into the microphone. "Loud and clear."

"Vanderer! Shut down your Drive. Heave to. Heave to. Do you vish to fall into the claws of Flight Marshal Phrymicki, of the Orbital Blockade? Ve have varned you . . ."

"Go and lay an egg!" retorted Tallentire rudely into the microphone. "Preferably a nice knobby one, like a pineapple."

There was a long silence while, presumably, the Hallichek linguist leafed through her dictionary to discover the meaning of Tallentire's simile. When she replied she used words that are not usually found in dictionaries, but that are included in the *lingua franca* of deep space.

"And I thought you were a lady . . ." sighed Tallentire sadly.

VIII

THIS WAS the first time that Trafford had ever made a close approach to a planet with his Mannschenn Drive in operation. *There has to be a first time for everything,* he thought grimly. *I hope it's not the last time for anything. . . .*

The ships of the Seventh Cruiser Squadron had abandoned the chase when still well clear of the Outer Van Allan Belt but, avarice at last superseded by intraservice loyalty, were now in full and open communication with the Orbital Blockade. The speakers of the Control Room transceivers made the air hideous with their squawkings and cluckings until Irene ordered them switched off. None of *Wanderer's* people was a good enough linguist to understand what was being said, but Metzenther, maintaining his telepathic listening watch, was able to keep his shipmates informed.

"The message," he whispered, "is 'Intercept! Intercept! Intercept those crazy loons before they destroy themselves!' "

And that's just what we could do, thought Trafford glumly. He knew now, as well as did Irene and Bronheim, the risks that were being taken. Allowance had been made for the orbit of every satellite circling Antrim—but there were bodies for which no allowance could be made—ships that had lifted from and put down on the planet in the recent past, and the vessels of the Orbital Blockade. *If we must have a collision,* he added mentally, *I hope that it's with one of the Hallichek cruisers. . . .*

"Captain!" Metzenther's voice was urgent. "Think positively. Think positively!"

"Damned eavesdropper!" growled Trafford, and Irene—who, with Bronheim, was crouched tensely over the remote controls of the Drive—looked up briefly and snapped, "What's all this about?"

"The Captain, ma'am. He's allowing himself to be pessimistic."

"We can't afford that, Benjamin. We've told you what to look out for. You have to take the ship through. Just do your best, that's all."

Yes, Trafford thought. *I know what to look out for. I've been told. But shall I recognize it when I see it?* He squared his shoulders. *I just damn well have to, that's all.*

Ahead, as seen through the wide viewport, the universe was crazy. It was not a sphere towards which they were falling at suicidal speed, but a ring of solid light, a vast, glowing annulus. And there were other circles of luminosity around it, intersecting it, an incredibly complex interlacing tracery, a multidimensional web that must surely trap the plunging ship to destroy her without trace and, at the same time, utterly devastate thousands of square miles of the surface of the world to which she was bringing succor.

It was a web, it was a net, and it was woven of the trajectories of other ships—peaceful merchantmen and Hallicheki cruisers—and of the fifty satellites in orbit about Antrim. *Wanderer*'s own trajectory, as computed by Irene, would take her clear of the metal and plastic moons, but there were still the warships and the tramps and the liners to be accounted for. And it was impossible to distinguish one trajectory from another.

The odds against a collision, even so, were astronomical. Violent contact between two bodies is an event in space/time, not in space alone. But Black Bart, the pirate, had taken the chance, and he had been unlucky. If the taking of such a chance could be avoided, then the chances of a successful conclusion to the voyage would be vastly improved.

It was a web, it was a net, and the strands of it were of

varying degrees of brightness. "Keep away from the bright trajectories," Irene had told him. "If you can."

If I can . . . he thought.

Directly ahead of *Wanderer* one such trajectory was an incandescent catenary in the haze, a cable of blue fire looping into infinity. It might be safe to pass through it, it might not. It didn't look safe. It looked too . . . solid. Trafford acted quickly. The Inertial Drive generators screamed as lateral thrust was applied with no preliminary slow-down of fore-and-aft impulsion. The maneuver could have wrecked a merchant vessel, but a warship was built to be able to withstand abnormal strains. The ship creaked and protested briefly, then shrugged off the racking stress. Some of her equipment was not so robust. Susanna cried out in alarm as the tank of the Mass Proximity Indicator exploded in a blue-white flare that was brighter even than the harsh radiance streaming through the ports.

She said shakily, "That was close."

"You're telling me," muttered Trafford, punching controls to bring the ship back on course.

"The M.P.I.'s had it."

"Too bad."

Through the gleaming web plunged *Wanderer,* through the maze of filaments that were the tracks of meteorites—and collision with the smallest of these could be as disastrous, insofar as the ship was concerned, as with another vessel—through the interlacing spirals of thick strands of luminosity that were the trajectories of ships and satellites.

At the Mannschenn Drive controls, Irene and Bronheim muttered to each other now and again, and once Irene swore. Their task was less spectacular than Trafford's, but it was at least as hard. The inventor of the Mannschenn Drive had never envisaged its operation in such a crowded volume of space. Even more hazardous than the seen dangers, the ones with which Trafford was coping, were the ones that registered only by oscilloscope. There was the interplay of vast forces, the enormous temporal weight of the planet, billions upon billions of year/tons, striving to crush this impudent intruder into conformity within the continuum.

And she was fighting back—not by brute strength, for her own machinery, mighty as it was, was less than a clockwork toy in comparison with the vast forces that powered the universe. She was fighting back with intelligence, with cunning, yielding a little so that she could slip away from between the jaws that were closing upon her, and then seizing every slight advantage that offered itself. She was slithering through the cracks in the fabric of space/time, a tiny, agile insect evading the forefinger and thumb that were poised to crush her, a fly whose random dartings took her out of the path of the cosmic fly swatter.

Ahead of them, close ahead, was Antrim. No longer was the planet a vast circle, a huge ring of mottled light. It was a green-gold plain that filled the viewports, an undulating plain, pulsing with an odd, disturbing slowness. It was like an amoeba, the ectoplasm of which was fluid luminescence. And it was matter. Solid, fluid, or semi-fluid, it made no difference. At *Wanderer's* speed, when she hit she would disintegrate, would become, in a microsecond, no more than a puff of incandescent metallic vapor. So Trafford thought, remembering that the first man to attempt this maneuver had never reached the actual surface of his planetary base. Then he remembered that Black Bart had been well inside the atmosphere when his ship had fouled the trajectory of the orbital fort, and that if *Wanderer* were in any danger of being destroyed by collision with the structure of the planet this would already have happened—at enormous speeds air was as solid as the side of a mountain. It was the trajectories that he still had to watch out for, the tracks of ships and satellites that, in space/time, passed through the track of the orbiting world.

They were below the surface now, and it was dark, but not so dark as Trafford had expected. The glowing filaments still persisted, the great, looping cables of luminosity. Again and again he had to use his lateral thrust; whether or not it was really necessary he did not know, but knew that if he did not do so when it was necessary he would never know anything anymore. And then came the worst part of it. A glare from outside filled the Control Room, the effulgence of the planet's internal fires. It was impossible to see, against the incandescence of molten rock and metal, the strands of the web. And there was the feeling of heat, of intolerable pressure. It was only an illusion, but it was more than unpleasant—it was terrifying.

Then there was the darkness again, and the curving, looping strands and filaments—and suddenly, seen through the mesh of the net, there were the glowing whorls of light that were the stars. They were through. They had plunged through the heart of the planet as though it were nonexistent, had fallen through into blessedly empty space, and astern of them, more distant with every passing second, was the night side of Antrim.

The Mass Proximity Indicator was out of commission, and the radar could not be used with the Mannschenn Drive in operation, so there was nothing for it but dead reckoning. Trafford had noted the time at which they had broken clear of the surface, was watching the sweep of the second hand on the console's clock.

"All right," he said at last. "Shut down the Drive."

"Captain," expostulated Metzenther. "The Hallicheki. One of their ships. Close, I think."

"Are they expecting us?"

"No."

"Good. Mr. Tallentire, stand by. A.M. action only."

"A.M. action only, sir." The Gunnery Officer sounded disappointed.

There was the usual disorientation as *Wanderer* dropped back into the normal continuum, the usual fleeting sensation of *déja vu*. And then the stars—hard, bright points of radiance were all around them, and below them was the night side of the planet, twinkling with the lights of towns and cities, the homes of men.

Susanna had switched on the transceivers, and from the speaker of one of them burst that infuriating squawking and clucking, followed by the words, in a psittacine voice, "*Vanderer! Vanderer!* Heave to!"

IX

THE HALLICHEK CRUISER was invisible in the darkness, in the long shadow of the planet, too far distant to show up in silhouette against the starry sky. She carried no lights But there was a bright pip in the tank that was *Wanderer's* radar screen, and a smaller pip that detached itself from its parent, that began to close the range between the two ships with ever mounting velocity. This, Trafford thought, would be the warning signal, the shot across the bows, with a proximity fuse that would detonate its warhead when it was a safe (but not overly safe) distance from the target. Evasion would be useless. As long as the rocket's fuel held out it could outrun a ship operating on Inertial Drive—especially a ship making a controlled fall towards a planetary surface—and it would home on any source of radiation.

"All right, Mr. Tallentire," said Trafford.

"No." It was Irene. "*No*. Do you want us all to be condemned as pirates? A man of war is entitled to fire a warning shot."

"How are we to know that it is one, ma'am?" asked the Gunnery Officer sarcastically.

"If it comes inside the legal proximity fuse setting we have grounds for assuming that it's not. In territorial Space that is—as far as I can remember—five kilometers . . ."

"It's going to pass ahead of us," announced Susanna, who had the radar watch. Then there was a sudden flare of intense brilliance. "It *was* going to pass ahead of us," she amended. "The burst was a good ten kilometers distant."

"Chemical, I'd say," contributed Tallentire. "Magnesium and oxygen . . ."

"*Vanderer*, heave to! Heave to! That vas a varning!"

Irene had the microphone in her hand. "I am sorry," she said, slowly and distinctly. "We cannot. Our Inertial Drive is malfunctioning. We shall be able to make a landing—we hope—but we are unable to throw ourselves into any sort of orbit."

"Heave to! Heave to! Or ve open fire!"

"Are you at war with the Empire?"

"No. But you are a smuggler. You vill be seized as a prize."

"We wear the colors of a merchant vessel of the Imperium," she said coldly. "We are proceeding on our lawful occasions."

"They're closing us," said Susanna. "Fast."

"They would be." Irene turned to face the others in the Control Room. "I'm going to try to provoke our friends into a slight breach of legality. For all they know, our story about the malfunctioning Inertial Drive is true. They are entitled to come alongside to board and investigate. But they are *not* entitled to open fire until we have made some obvious attempt at escape. So far we have not. We are falling sedately towards the surface of Antrim, at such a speed that they can overtake and board with ease before we're anywhere near the outer limits of the exosphere. Until it's proved otherwise, we're little, innocent woolly lambs. If *they* start something, it puts *us* in a good light. Relatively speaking."

"They're within effective laser range," said Susanna.

"Mr. Tallentire," Irene told him, "anti-missile missiles and anti-missile laser in readiness. Also the anti-laser smokescreen." She released her pressure on the microphone stud, the controlling switch of the instrument that she had covered with her hand, so that the transceiver functioned as a receiver.

"Calling *Vanderer!*" squawked the Hallichek voice. "Calling *Vanderer* . . ."

"We hear you, loud and clear. Come in, please."

"*Vanderer,* stand by to be taken in tow. Stand by to receive our boarding party."

"Standing by, standing by. But be sure you have a good dust bath to get the lice out of your feathers before you board our ship."

The speaker erupted into raucous squawking. For every nation and for every race there are fighting words—and when a race is so notoriously emotionally unstable as the Hallichek such words may be relied upon to start a fight.

Tallentire laughed happily, swept his hand over his firing keys. From vents in *Wanderer's* sleek sides gushed the expanding cloud of highly reflective vapors, a screen that would mask her own laser projectors but still leave them fairly effective at short range, effective enough to dispose of any Hallichek rockets that got past the anti-missile missiles, a screen that would shield her from anything more serious than a slight heating of the shell plating, unless the enemy got to almost within boarding distance.

But the Hallicheki would not; Trafford was making sure of that. *Wanderer* was no longer falling towards Antrim, her Inertial Drive slowing the rate of descent. She was being driven down to the planet by the full power of her engines.

Calmly and coldly Irene was speaking into the microphone. "*Wanderer* to Hallichek cruiser. *Wanderer* to Hallichek cruiser. I shall report this act of unprovoked aggression to the Imperial Ambassador on Antrim, also to your own Ambassador. You deliberately fired on my ship, at a time when we were preparing to receive your inspecting officers."

A new voice crackled from the speaker in reply, less excitable, and almost as cold as Irene's own. "You vere lying. Your Drive is not malfunctioning. You are trying to evade capture."

"We are now—and with good reason. Do you expect us to be a sitting duck for your gunners?"

"Heave to. There vill be no more shooting—unless *you* provoke *us* again."

"What do you take us for, duckie?" (And that, Trafford knew, was far from being a term of endearment among the Hallichecki.) "Once bitten, twice shy." She glanced at Trafford, who was anxiously watching his instruments, read his expression. "Furthermore, we are already in the exosphere. We are in Antrim territorial atmosphere, and subject to the laws of that planet. Over," she said simply. "And *out.*"

Trafford, listening to her, was annoyed by her smugness. To slow the ship before her skin was heated to incandescence by atmospheric friction would not be easy. He threw the Drive into full reverse, winced at the scream of tortured machinery, the groaning complaints of structural members. But it was not enough. Both air-speed indicators and ship-to-surface radar showed a terrifying rate of descent. There was only one thing for it—the emergency rockets. The sudden deceleration threw him back into his chair, slammed him deep into the padding. Livid exhaust fire washed up around the ports. And Metzenther, speaking in a quiet voice that somehow carried above the screaming thunder, remarked, "They are very happy. They think that we have blown up."

"We're not far from it," muttered Trafford.

X

INDEED, they were not far from it. Neither the Inertial Drive nor the emergency rockets alone could possibly have braked their steep descent in time, and their simultaneous employment was almost disastrous. Almost disastrous, too, was the initial rate of their fall through the upper atmosphere. The pumps labored to maintain the flow of coolant through the space between inner and outer shells, and the internal temperature rose sharply.

The maneuver had been hard on the ship—and harder still on her personnel. Luckily for them they were all well trained; they all knew better than to leave their acceleration chairs during any sort of action—but, even so, some of them had been taken unawares by the sudden, violent deceleration, had been thrown back and down into the deep padding in awkward, contorted attitudes.

When, at last, Trafford had the ship under control again, when the crushing weight on his body had eased and it was possible to cut the reaction drive, he was able to look around him. Irene was all right (she would be) and returned his anxious, questioning look with a confident smile. Bronheim looked as stolid as always, but his face was not as ruddy as usual. Metzenther was sprawled in his chair, face gray and breathing ragged. He opened his eyes, read the question on Trafford's face and muttered, "Just shaken. That's all." Tallentire was white and trembling, but had eyes only for Susanna, who seemed to be unconscious. A thin trickle of blood from the corner of her mouth was very dark against her face.

"You can see to her, Mr. Tallentire," Trafford told him.

Unsteadily, the Gunnery Officer got up from his chair,

weaved towards the girl. He knelt beside her, whispering her name, repeated it in a louder voice. And then Irene took charge. Not ungently, she half lifted and half pushed him to one side. She ran expert hands over Susanna's limbs and body. She said brusquely, "I don't think that there's anything broken, Mr. Tallentire. If you'll get some cold water ..."

The speaker of the transceiver came to life. A blessedly human voice said, "Aerospace Control calling unknown ship. Is that you, *Wanderer?* Come in, please."

The sound of the strange voice stirred Susanna to wakefulness. Her eyes opened, she stretched out a hand and lifted a microphone from its clip. "*Wanderer* to Aerospace Control. Have you anything for us? Over."

"Have we anything for you? We're damn glad to see you, that's all. But what is your condition? Do you require assistance? Can you make it to Port Donegal?"

"What shall I tell them, ma'am?" asked the girl.

"This is your baby, Benjamin," said Irene to Trafford.

Trafford scanned his instruments. It would not have been correct to say that all machinery was functioning perfectly—but everything *was* functioning. The Inertial Drive, which had taken the worst hammering, was holding up well. Speed was down to a comfortable six hundred knots and the overheating of the shell had ceased.

"Tell them," he said, "that we are under full control. Ask them for instructions."

Susanna did so, and the voice of the controller, now calm and businesslike, instructed them to follow the beam to Port Donegal.

And so *Wanderer* sped over the dark countryside, the lights of towns and cities sliding away beneath her. She was heading east, and when the sun came up it seemed to leap into the sky. The world revealed by the golden light was a fair one—blue lakes set among green mountains, mile after mile of golden beach along the shore of an indigo sea. It was a world that had been spared the worst ravages of industrialization, of overpopulation, and the plumes of white smoke and steam drifting from the stacks of the infrequent factories served only to enhance the beauty of their natural surroundings.

Then there was Port Donegal—low, silvery buildings and a lofty latticework control tower set in a vast, lawn-like expanse. There was Port Donegal, and the voice of the controller was replaced by another feminine one, a voice that made no attempt to be unemotional, businesslike. "This is the Minister of Health, *Wanderer*. We never thought you'd make it. But you have, you have, and we shall be eternally grateful to you. This world is yours, *Wanderer*, as long as you wish to stay here."

"And we may have to stay here longer than we wish," remarked Irene. "We got down—but shall we be allowed to get back up?"

XI

"BUT SURELY, sir," said Tallentire, "we should be able to get away from Antrim the same way as we got to it. With you as pilot, and with Her Imperial Highness and Commander Bronheim at the Mannschenn Drive controls . . ."

"And with you to play a solo, as required, on the console of your battle organ . . ." added Trafford. And then he looked at his officer severely. "Mr. Tallentire, must I remind you yet again that you signed on as Second Mate, and that the Second Mate of a merchantman is the navigator? Come to that, must I also remind you that the only rank held by Mrs. Trafford is that of Mate of this vessel; she is no longer Her Imperial Highness—and the fewer people who hear you referring to her in those words, the better. Anyhow, *you* are the navigator. On paper, at least. As such you should have some rough idea as to what the Interstellar Drive can and can *not* do.

"Our somewhat unorthodox approach maneuver succeeded for only one reason: after a long voyage we had built up enough momentum, just barely enough to carry us through the millions of years of temporal inertia possessed by a planet such as this. *But* we cannot start from cold on a planetary surface. Furthermore, even if we could, we should soon find ourselves in trouble. Within a second we should have violated that well-known law of physics, the one that states that two solid bodies cannot occupy the same position at the same time. So . . ."

"So what do we do, sir? Oh, I know that there would be far worse worlds than this to be marooned upon, and once the antibiotics we brought have the plague licked it will be very pleasant indeed." His manner brightened. "But sooner or later the Hallicheki will forget about this confrontation business, and I shall be able to get back to my proper work."

"It's a damn pity that you didn't get a dose of hallucinogens with the rest of us," Trafford told him. "Then you wouldn't be so keen on shooting and being shot at."

"But we're mercenaries, sir," pointed out Tallentire. "And shooting is the main part of the mercenary's trade."

While Trafford was considering his reply, he heard Irene calling from just outside the wardroom door, "Come on, Benjamin. Have you forgotten that we're going to give Their Excellencies a piece of our minds? You'll have plenty of time to play at spacemanship instructor when we get back to the ship."

"Don't keep Her Imperial Highness waiting . . ." murmured Tallentire.

The drive from the spaceport to the city was a pleasant one, so pleasant that all the passengers in the hired car, with the possible exception of Irene, were sorry that the vehicle was capable of such a high rate of speed. The day was fine and warm, and the air was heavy with the scent of the great banks of flowering shrubs—some familiar, native to Earth and the earlier colonized planets, some of local origin—that bordered the long, straight road. Beyond this high, blossoming hedge could be glimpsed orchards—row after row of fruit trees drawn up with military precision—and green fields where cattle grazed, Jerseys and Frisians whose ancestors had been deep-frozen ova in *Lode Antrim's* holds. Beyond the fields and the orchards were the blue hills, hardly deeper in tone than the blue sky, where great cloud galleons, towering cumuli, slowly drifted.

At first the only signs of human habitation were the white farmhouses. They were like ships riding the low, green swells, each with its suit of sail, and gleaming, solar power screens. And then the car was skimming through the suburbs, past villas, each of which stood in its own wide garden, through beautifully landscaped parks, across a graceful bridge that spanned a wide river. But in spite of the fineness of the day, there were few people abroad, only a very occasional vehicle, a mere scattering of pedestrians. The car had slowed now, and Trafford was able to look at the faces of the colonists whom they passed. All of them were listless, apathetic. All of them were marked by strain and sickness. These, the lucky ones, could be saved by the medicines in *Wanderer's* cargo—but there must be many, far too many, for whom the blockade runner had come too late.

They were in the city now, rolling along a wide avenue past gracious buildings built of the local limestone, so proportioned as to call to mind the architecture of ancient Greece. There were no skyscrapers, no towering aboveground warrens, only the occasional tower of a church or public hall to reach up into the sky. It was, thought Trafford, a *quiet* city, and it would still be a quiet city when all its population had been restored to health, when the census had once again increased to its pre-plague level.

At last the car slowed to a halt outside a long, low colonnaded structure, gleaming whitely behind the elaborate wrought-iron railings and the high gateway, in which was displayed the winged, crowned sphere, the arms of Imperial Earth. From a flagstaff on top of the building floated a dark blue flag that carried the same device. Inside the gateway, between it and the high bronze door, a quartet of sentries paced with slow regularity, wearing uniforms of blue and gold, with glittering and utterly unfunctional bayonets affixed to the muzzles of their laser rifles—each man a credit to Her Imperial Highness's Corps of Marines.

"I never did like those bastards," muttered Her ex-Imperial Highness.

"They have their uses," Trafford told her.

A sergeant emerged from the doorway, strutted along the drive, waited until one of the sentries opened the gate for him. He walked importantly to the car. He gave a salute that was correct, but that somehow conveyed the impression of courtesy reluctantly accorded to mere civilians. He asked, "Captain Trafford and his officers?" And then, when Trafford had replied in the affirmative, said, "His Excellency is waiting for you."

Trafford was first out of the monowheel, then helped Irene to alight. The sergeant stared at her, then stiffened. The spaceman could almost read the soldier's thoughts. *This can't possibly be the Empress—but I'd better be careful.* The Marine saluted again, with a snap that had been lacking from his first attempt, this time looking warily at Trafford. *Merchant skipper perhaps,* were his almost audible thoughts, *but this joker has an Imperial Navy cut to his jib. . . .* He said, "Sir, will you and the ladies and the other gentlemen please follow me?"

Inside the gateway the sentries smartly presented arms, no doubt warned by a gesture from the N.C.O.

The party followed the sergeant into the Embassy—Trafford and Irene first, Susanna and Metzenther bringing up the rear. They walked along high-ceilinged corridors, over a floor of beautifully grained wood polished to a mirror finish. There was an air of luxury, of opulence, throughout. It was obvious that Her Imperial Highness's Ambassador to Antrim did himself well, very well. Trafford was not surprised when he met that gentleman himself, a portly and rubicund individual, white-maned and white-mustachioed, seated in his big, tapestry-hung office behind a huge, leather-covered desk. He got to his feet reluctantly when he saw Trafford, then with a show of alacrity when the women entered. The look he bestowed upon Susanna was more of a leer than anything else. But when he looked at Irene there was a hint of puzzlement on his fat features, a flicker of uncertainty behind the protuberant blue eyes.

"Captain Trafford?" he asked unnecessarily.

"Yes, Your Excellency. Allow me to introduce Mrs. Trafford, my Chief Officer, Miss Weldon, my Purser, and Mr. Metzenther, my Communications Officer."

The Ambassador grunted acknowledgement, then said, "Please be seated." He glared at Trafford across his desk. "I suppose you realize, Captain, that you have placed me in a very embarrassing situation."

"I had imagined, Your Excellency, that your stocks on this planet must be high at the moment. After all, we have broken the blockade and brought sorely needed medical supplies to Antrim."

"Hrumph. Yes. Yes. You have broken the blockade. And the way in which you did it—the mere fact that you have done it—puts Earth in a very bad light. Let me tell you, young man, that thanks to your illegal activities I am having to bat on a very sticky wicket. Yes. Very sticky. And my naval attaché advises me that not only did you hazard your own ship but could easily have caused widespread devastation on the surface of this world. But these matters of spacemanship I leave to the technicians. What concerns me directly is that you have alienated the Hallicheki. It will be a long, uphill task for me to restore friendly relations between the Empire and the Hegemony. . . ."

"My heart fair bleeds for you," condoled Irene.

"What? What was that, madam?"

"You heard me, Your Excellency. And now hear this. We are here to enter a formal complaint against your feathered friends. The action that they took against our ship, a peacable merchantman wearing the colors of Imperial Earth, proceeding on her lawful occasions, was tantamount to piracy.

We were fired upon—and I don't mean just a warning shot across the bows either. We were fired upon, and only speed and the Master's spacemanship saved us from total destruction. We were fired upon without provocation."

"Sir," snapped the Ambassador, bristling, "I must ask you to control your officer."

"My Mate," said Trafford mildly, "did no more than say, though in somewhat stronger terms, what I was about to say."

"And so you wish to lodge a complaint?"

"Too right we do," answered Irene.

The diplomat swelled visibly. "It may interest you to know," he blustered, "that a complaint has already been lodged by the Hallichek Ambassador about yourselves." He checked off the points on his pudgy fingers. "One—you are guilty of smuggling. Two—you refused to 'heave to' when ordered so to do by a competent authority. Three—on two occasions you were guilty of using grossly insulting language to the commanders of Hallicheki warships. Four—you actually fired on a Hallicheki warship." He looked almost happy as he murmured his concluding words. "Smuggling *and* piracy."

"In other words," Irene told him, wiping the gloating expression from his face, "not, repeat not, cricket. But confrontation, Your Excellency, is no more a game than war is—or if it is, it's a damned dirty one."

"Watch your language, young woman." A telephone on his desk buzzed. He picked it up. "Very well," he said into the instrument. "I shall be pleased to receive her." Then, to the party from *Wanderer,* "Her Excellency, the Hallichek Ambassadress, wishes to make a further complaint to you in person."

XII

TRAFFORD HAD NEVER, until this moment, met a member of the avian race—but as a naval officer he had sat through the instructional films that were supposed to familiarize their viewers with the appearance of every intelligent life form in the known galaxy, the Hallicheki included. But the films and the solidographs had been inadequate preparation for the actual experience.

To begin with, there was the smell—an acridity of dry, never-washed feathers, plus the aroma of fowl manure. And there was the physical presence of the creature. It clattered into the Ambassador's office arrogantly, the talons of its huge, splayed feet scarring the polished floor. On its stiltlike, scaly legs it stood all of eight feet high. Its general appearance was not unlike that of a Terran ostrich—but the wings, each bearing at its tip a manipulatory claw, seemed to be functional. The plumage was drab—a dusty brown, against which a great jewel hung on a thick golden chain from the long neck, glowing balefully.

The saucerlike eyes glowed balefully too. They were set on either side of a wattled beak, and they stared unwinkingly at each of the occupants of the room in turn. When it was his turn to be inspected, Trafford met the cold glare unflinchingly, studied the face of the Ambassadress. There was little of the ostrich about that head. It was more that of a barnyard fowl, and the expression of the avian features was spiteful, vindictive. *It*, thought Trafford (he still could not think of the Hallichek as "she"), *must rank high in the pecking order of its tribe.* But above the eyes the skull bulged, where it housed the brain of a creature capable of building and maintaining an interstellar civilization. And the beak was the cruel beak of a bird of prey.

"Your Excellency," murmured the Terran Ambassador respectfully.

"Your Excellency," squawked the Ambassadress in reply.

"Your Excellency, may I introduce Captain Trafford and his officers?"

"Ah. The pirates."

"The blockade runners," corrected Trafford coldly. "Not that we admit the legality of your blockade."

"Pirates!" screeched the Ambassadress. "Smugglers! You fired upon the *Kerestrel!* Your lives are forfeit!"

"*Kerestrel* fired upon us," said Trafford. "We were obliged to bring our anti-missile and anti-laser defenses into play."

"And this *Vanderer* is a peaceful merchant vessel. Yet she mounts the armament of a light cruiser!"

Irene broke in. "Madam, high-ranking representatives of your Hegemony were among the signatories of the Treaty of Capella. Among its many clauses is one that clearly defines the right of merchantmen to carry defensive weapons at all times and in all sectors, whether or not a state of war exists. The actual definition of defensive armament is somewhat vague."

"*I* say you are pirates. Flight Marshal Phrymicki says you are pirates. Flight Marshal Krakeka says you are pirates and smugglers. I have already presented a demand for your extradition to the President of Antrim."

"And if, by any strange chance, we are extradited?" asked Trafford.

The Ambassadress seemed to have lost interest in him. She contorted her long neck, looked down to the feathers on her breast. There was something crawling there, something whose color matched that of the plumage in which it had made its home, but with a shiny carapace. The hooked beak opened and darted down with the speed of a striking snake, snapped shut. There was a sharp crack. The bird head came erect, the play of the muscles of the long neck showed that something was being swallowed. The Hallichek looked again at Trafford and clucked smugly, "*That!*"

Irene broke the shocked silence. She turned to the Ambassador. "And you have the crust to tell us that you wish to remain on friendly terms with these verminous creatures!"

The Ambassador flushed angrily, looking something like a turkey cock himself. "Control your insolence, young woman. Since when has the Mate of a star tramp been qualified to question the workings of Imperial policy?"

"You'd be surprised," she told him, with acid sweetness, and his flush faded and the uneasiness flickered again behind his eyes. "You'd be surprised."

"And as for *you*," squawked the Hallichek to the Ambassador, "vhat the hell are you playing at? Am *I*, the accredited representative of the Hegemony, to be insulted in your coop, on Terran territory, by these scavengers of Space?"

"But, Your Excellency . . ."

"It vas a mistake. I said so, in Council. It vas a mistake ever to think ve could deal vith *mammals*." She made the word sound like an insult. ".I shall send my report. I shall make my recommendations." She paused. "And if this should mean var—then you vill be to blame!"

She clattered indignantly from the office.

"Who are you?" asked the Ambassador plaintively. "Who *are* you?"

"Mrs. Irene Trafford. Chief Officer of the merchant vessel *Wanderer*. Chief Officer *and* owner."

The fat man looked at her dubiously. He said, "When I was in legal practice I had occasional dealings with Terran merchant shipping. And, in my experience, Mates don't usually own the vessels they serve in. . . ."

"There has to be a first time," she told him.

"Yes, I suppose so. But . . ."

"But what?"

"That portrait on the wall. Her Imperial Highness, the Empress Irene. You're a little fuller in the face, perhaps, a little more . . . muscular?"

"Masseroni always tended to idealize his subjects."

"Then you *are* . . . ?"

"I am *not*. Even so, Mr. Ambassador, I do know something of the workings of Imperial policy."

"Oh," said the man, "I begin to see. You're one of the stand-ins."

"Could be. Could be not. But, take it from me, the Hallicheki daren't risk war. They're too dependent upon the Empire for various manufactured goods, mainly machinery, which they can't make themselves. Too, once you let yourself get pecked, you're on your way down to the bottom of the pecking order. And that you can't afford."

The Ambassador managed a grin. He said to Trafford, "You seem to have rather an unusual Chief Officer, Captain."

"You can say that again," Trafford told him. "But all my officers are quite well qualified. My Communications Officer, for example, holds a Rhine Institute diploma. We should not be speaking so freely to you if he had not given us the assurance, telepathically, that you were to be trusted." *Up to a point,* he added mentally. "Of course, the invasion of psychological privacy is a breach of the Institute's rules, but now and again an occasion that warrants it will arise."

"And did you read the thoughts of Her Excellency?" asked the Ambassador.

"Yes," answered Metzenther. "She's just trying it on. She knows that the President would never consent to our extradition, and she knows, too, that her superiors would take a very dim view of any breaking off of diplomatic relations with the Empire. Insofar as Antrim is concerned, the policy is one of confrontation. There is the underlying fear that a declaration of war against this world would mean a large scale conflict with the Empire."

"But what am I to do?" wailed the Ambassador.

"Don't let yourself be pecked," snapped Irene. "Just remember that you represent us, that you're supposed to be protecting us against that flock of vultures waiting to pounce on the carcass of this world."

The man smiled feebly. "I rather gained the impression that you people were well able to protect yourselves."

"One ship against a fleet? And, sir, even we have to consider legalities, the use of armament against a vessel wearing the flag of a nation with which one's own nation is not at war is piracy."

"So you admit it."

"When we ran the blockade we used anti-missile and anti-laser weapons only. We aren't pirates yet."

"If you have to fight your way clear of Antrim you may well be," said the Ambassador, with a certain glum satisfaction.

XIII

AFTER LEAVING the Embassy, and before calling on the President, they found a quiet tavern and, in its cool, dark-paneled saloon bar, sat down to discuss matters over silver tankards of dark, tangy stout.

"If that creature was typical of the Hallicheki," muttered Susanna, "I'm even sorrier that Tallentire wasn't allowed to play a real symphony on his battle organ!" She sipped her drink thoughtfully. "But it doesn't make sense. There was that *filthy* business with the louse or whatever it was—and yet those birds in the cruiser really flew off the handle when you told them to delouse themselves before boarding our ship."

Irene laughed. "The personnel of the Hallichek Navy, like the spacemen of other races, are somewhat fanatical on the subject of personal cleanliness. They despise the non-space-farers for their scruffiness. But to beings like the Ambassadress the occasional parasite plucked from their own plumage is like a salted peanut is to us." She turned to Metzenther. "Well, Commander, you were flapping your psionic ears. What did you learn?"

"To begin with," said the telepath, "there was the Ambassador. You had him worried. A good Mate should be an arrogant bastard—but you were more arrogant than the norm. And then, of course, there was your appearance. I've no doubt that the Empress Irene has quite a few doubles throughout the Galaxy, but when you started playing hell with a big stick . . .

"Anyhow, you threw a scare into him. He's thinking that perhaps he has been a little too pro-Hallichek, and that his future advancement might suffer in consequence."

"But I just can't see how any human could be pro-Halli-chek in these circumstances," protested Trafford. "Surely he's not frightened of them."

It was Irene who answered. "It may surprise you, Benjamin, to learn that a good deal of thought goes into the appointment of ambassadors. To take one obvious example, an aelurophobe would be most unsuitable to represent the Empire among a felinoid people. Our friend whom we have just left is one of those who were handpicked for service in the Hallichek sector. If my memory serves me right, his main qualification is that he is an ornithologist of note. Strange though it may seem, in his dealings with the Hallicheki he is motivated by love, not by fear."

"Yes," confirmed Metzenther. "That was the impression I gained—although it puzzled me that a human should evince such a strange, almost parental affection for that unpleasant old hen."

"So he loves the Hallicheki and fears you," said Trafford.

"That's about the size of it. Now, I'm going to give you another slight surprise. In addition to being an ornithologist, our friend is—or was, until his appointment—a well-known lawyer, specializing in Space Law. The moral, of course, is never let appearances mislead you. The man's no fool. I think that he just might be able to figure out a way in which we can get off this world, shooting our way out without doing more than bending the law. I've the glimmerings of an idea myself. . . ."

"Which is?" Trafford asked.

"I'd rather not say, until I'm sure of my ground." She drained her mug, then said, "We'll have another round, and then we'll make our call on the President."

They walked from the tavern to the Presidential Palace, the dignified white building from whose flagstaff flew the green flag with its golden harp. At the gates they did not have to produce any identification; they were recognized and in a matter of seconds a guard of honor of green-uniformed soldiers was drawn up. Trafford was amused by Irene's resentment, brief though it was, when he, as the senior officer present, took the salute. The soldiers escorted them to the main doorway of the palace, where they were received by a man in naval uniform, wearing commodore's braid. After the exchange of courtesies the Commodore conducted them to the President's office.

President McGowan was a little man, wiry, his seamed face dark above the high, starched collar of his archaic morning dress. He rose to his feet as they entered the room, came from behind his desk and shook hands cordially with each one of them. The Commodore fussed around arranging chairs for them, then produced a decanter and glasses.

When they were settled down, the President said, "It's eternally grateful we all are to ye, Captain. Thanks to you—and to our good friends of GLASS—the epidemic's licked." He frowned. "But now ye're here, what are we to do with ye?"

"Enlist them in our Navy," suggested the Commodore. "We could use their ship, too."

"Now, now, Timothy. There's no call for ye to be playin' the recruitin' sergeant. Not this early in the game." The President twirled the stem of his glass between his gnarled fingers. "Frankly, Captain, ye're a slight embarrassment to us. The Hallicheki are milling around like a mob of wet hens, an' that auld biddie of an Ambassadress has practically been layin' eggs on my doorstep ever since ye berthed. 'Tis extradition they're demandin'. Needless to say, they're demandin' the impossible. But, first of all, d'ye want to stay on Antrim? We can find jobs for ye in the Navy. . . ."

"Thank you for the offer, Mr. President," Irene told him,

"but this tramping, this free-lancing, is our way of life. We like your world, but we wouldn't like to be stuck for too long in one place." She added, as much for Trafford's benefit as the Commodore's, "After all, the Navy's no place for a real spaceman." A smile took the sting from her words.

"I see your point, Mrs. Trafford," said the President. "But I have to weigh the consequences of whatever you do. We'll suppose that ye lift from Antrim . . . then, as soon as ye're clear of the atmosphere, and before ye can start up the Interstellar Drive, the Hallecheki orbital blockade will pounce on ye. Ye can fight back, I know. But what then? Your ship is a Terran ship, an' the Hallicheki might well consider your piratical action a valid excuse for breaking off diplomatic relations with the Empire. An' if they do—where does that leave us? We aren't legally part of the Empire, but ever since the Hallicheki found us, we've been sheltering behind the guns of Earth."

"Haven't the Hallicheki already a war on their hands?" asked Irene. "I seem to recall that for quite some time there's been a squabble between their central government and a group of colonies that has declared itself autonomous."

"That is true, Mrs. Trafford. In fact you must have noticed those Hallicheki ships berthed not far from you at the spaceport—three merchantmen and a couple of corvettes wearing the colors of the Kokrel Federation, as they call themselves. They've been here . . ." He looked enquiringly towards his naval aide.

"Almost a year," contributed the Commodore. "They were unlucky. They managed to sneak in unobserved, to load a cargo of grain. They could have made their getaway, but just then the Hallicheki commenced their policy of confrontation against us, and the orbital blockade was instituted a day before they were ready for departure."

"But surely the Ambassadress would have reported their arrival," said Trafford.

"She did, eventually. But at the time that the Kokreli ships landed there was a major breakdown of our Carlotti Communications station. We weren't taking sides," he added virtuously, "but the Kokreli are more our sort of people, even though they are birds, than the Hallicheki."

"I thought they were members of the same race," objected Trafford.

"Oh, they are, they are. But on the Kokreli worlds the males have gained the ascendancy."

"And is that so much better?" asked Irene coldly.

"Yes," replied the Commodore firmly.

"I'll not argue about it now," she told him. She held out her empty glass suggestively, finally receiving a refill. "Thank you. Now, my memory may be at fault. I've rather lost touch with interstellar affairs of late. But I think that the Empire has recognized Kokrel. . . ."

"That is correct, Mrs. Trafford," said the President.

"Have the Kokreli a representative on this world?"

"They have so."

"Better and better."

"What are you driving at, Irene?" asked her husband.

"Legalities, legalities . . ." she murmured. "Legalities, and the thorough grounding in Terran history which I was given when I . . ." She noticed the puzzlement on the faces of the President and the Commodore, said hastily, "No matter."

"You seem to have an exceptional Chief Officer, Captain," the Commodore remarked to Trafford.

"Everybody tells me that, sir. I'm getting to the stage of almost believing it myself."

"Pipe down!" she snapped. "Now, Mr. President. I'd like you to arrange a meeting between ourselves, the Terran Ambassador, and the local top cookie of the Kokreli, whatever he calls himself."

"The Agent General," said the Commodore.

"As long as he has the power to act for his government, that's all that matters," said Irene.

XIV

MENTALLY TRAFFORD STILL referred to the Hallichek Ambassadress as "it," but the Kokrel Agent General was indubitably "he." He was a gorgeous figure, the plumage of his wings and back and fan-shaped tail was irridescent blue, that of the breast a gleaming gold with a rainbow spattering of feathers which, even at second glance, looked like the ribbons of decorations. The cruel head was topped by a flamboyant scarlet comb, and the natural spurs of the feet were sheathed in wickedly glittering steel. The overall effect was that of a full-dress uniform. He looked, in fact, more like a general than an agent.

He's an arrogant bastard, thought Trafford, *but he hasn't the petty spitefulness of the females of his species.*

They were in the Terran Ambassador's library: the Ambassador himself, the party from the ship, the President, the Commodore, and the Agent General. The humans were seated, the avian remained standing. The walls of the huge room were lined with books, heavy, leather-bound volumes that exuded an atmosphere of old-world dignity.

Irene subjected her surroundings to a scornful glance. She remarked, "You are fortunate, sir, that Ambassadorial effects are shipped at government expense. The freight on this mass of archaic paper must have been fantastically heavy."

"And would you have me stock my library with tapes and microfilms?" The Ambassador made them sound like dirty words. "Such gadgets, madam, detract from the essential dignity of the law."

"Yes, yes . . . You were a lawyer, were you not, before your appointment?"

"And not without fame, madam, in my own limited field.

I take it that it is upon some obscure point of Space Law that you wish to consult me." He added rather nastily, "It must be an *obscure* point, as I am sure that such a competent officer as yourself must be well versed in routine spatial legalities. And illegalities."

"Too right," she said cheerfully.

The Ambassador turned to the President and the Agent General. "And you, sirs, are also interested in the matter of the alleged freighter *Wanderer?*"

"That's the way of it, Mr. Ambassador," said the President, and the Agent General squawked, "Yes."

"So." The Ambassador looked at each of them in turn. "What do you have in mind?"

It was Irene who answered him. "To begin with, a state of war exists between the Kokrel Federation and the Hegemony. Secondly, there are Kokreli ships on this planet, trapped here by the orbital blockade. Regarding that, there is one small point that puzzles me. Antrim is neutral. As a neutral power, she can give harborage to merchantmen, but not to warships. And yet two of the Kokreli vessels are corvettes."

The Ambassador smiled coldly. "I have already been consulted on that point, Mrs. Trafford. By Her Excellency, as a matter of fact. Although those corvettes are owned by their government they are, officially, merchant vessels. Each has loaded a small, token cargo of grain. Their crews have signed standard mercantile Articles of Agreement. Their armament is defensive only." He added, with a touch of sarcasm, "Just as yours is."

The tall avian entered the discussion. "Mrs. Trafford's ship is, at the moment, unemployed. I wish to charter it, to carry a cargo of grain to Karakalla. Our own ships have also loaded for that world."

"I am no expert on naval matters," the Ambassador said,

"but it seems to me that getting clear of this planet will present certain problems. Your ships, even the corvettes, are only lightly armed. The blockading cruisers mount far superior fire power."

"Ve hope," replied the Agent General, "that *Vanderer's* fire power vill be the decisive factor."

"But *Wanderer* is a neutral vessel. She may not fire upon the warships of a belligerent power, even in self-defense."

"But, Mr. Ambassador, there are precedents for just that," Irene told him.

"Indeed, madam? I can recall none."

"Not, perhaps, in space warfare. But in war at sea. On Earth. About the middle of the Twentieth Century."

"Hitler's War?"

"Yes. Hitler's War."

"Go on," the Ambassador told her, interested. "Go on."

"It's something I stumbled upon during a course of historical studies. Just one of those small footnotes to history that nonetheless, can be quite fascinating. And this one stuck in my memory.

"Hitler's War, as you all know, was the first *scientific* war. There was widespread use of electronic devices, and missiles were used that were direct ancestors of the first spaceships. At the finish, nuclear weapons were employed. Also, it was the first war in which considerable use was made of air power.

"There were not many neutrals, but among the neutral powers was Sweden. The Swedes owned a considerable merchant fleet, and their ships, with Swedish flags painted on their topsides and superstructure, sailed in the big convoys that plied between the United States and England. In spite of their display of national colors they were often fired upon by the German aircraft that attacked the convoys. And there is nothing more annoying that being shot at without having the wherewithal to shoot back. The Swedish mariners didn't like it.

"Finally, some unsung genius came up with an answer to the problem. Of course, the ships could not mount armament that was the property either of their own government or of the British or American Admiralties. But . . .

"It was then, and is now, perfectly legal for Masters and Officers to carry weapons for their own protection. Normally, such weapons are only side arms—but there is nothing laid down in black and white. So the Swedish ships did, at the end, carry machine guns—*and* these guns, legally speaking, were the personal property of each Captain and his Mates. They signed receipts for them. Those point thirties or point three-oh-threes or whatever were private property, not government issue."

"H'm. But private individuals, Mrs. Trafford, don't own long-range laser projectors and missile batteries. Not even shipowners."

"This shipowner does, Mr. Ambassador. You may check my papers, if you wish. Should you do so, you will find that every item of equipment on *Wanderer*, including her armament, is my own personal property. Should I fire upon anybody in my own defense, it will be with *my* guns, not the Imperial Government's."

"You could still be classed as a pirate by the Hallicheki."

"If they did so, they'd be on somewhat shaky legal grounds."

"All wartime legalities are shaky," said the Ambassador sadly. "I have little doubt that if the Axis powers had won the war, those amateur Swedish machine gunners would have been tried and hanged as pirates."

"But this var the Hallicheki vill not vin," squawked the Agent General.

The Ambassador stared at him with distaste, said, "Sir, they have superiority of numbers."

"That is their only superiority. Vithout that . . ."

"I hope you do win," Irene said. "Meanwhile, all that I want to know is if we have found a legal way to use *Wanderer*'s armament in her own defense and in the defense of the Kokrel convoy."

"Very 'dubious legality," admitted the Ambassador grudgingly.

"But we're keeping the yardarm of the Imperial Government clear."

"The expression is a strange one, madam, but I think I see what you are driving at. Yes."

"Good. Finally, I wish to request that you divulge nothing whatsoever of what has transpired at this meeting to the Ambassadress."

The Agent General contrived to rattle his steel spurs suggestively on the polished floor, and hissed, "If he does . . ."

"Sir," remonstrated the Ambassador, "there is no call for threats of physical violence. In this matter I have acted as a legal adviser rather than as a plenipotentiary, and therefore am bound to observe the utmost secrecy. Mrs. Trafford will receive my account before her departure from Antrim—and I request you, Mr. President, to see to it that her vessel does not lift from the surface of this world until the account has been settled."

"No matter who wins a war," said the President, "the lawyers are always on the winning side!"

"He was speaking the truth, ma'am," said Metzenther, when they were back aboard the ship. "He likes the Hallicheki and he doesn't like the Kokreli, but he's our lawyer and as such must conform to legal ethics."

"Then you'd better arrange for the loading of this token grain cargo," Irene told Trafford.

"You're the Mate," he said. "Cargo is *your* concern."

"Stowage—yes. But you, my dear, have to sign the Charter Party. You have to do all the off-ship dickering."

"But this is all strange to me. . . ."

"Then it's time you learned. I'm too busy to attend to these things. I have to go into a huddle with our alleged Second Mate regarding the use and abuse of our allegedly defensive armament."

XV

ESPIONAGE IS comparatively easy when the spy can mingle with the people upon whom he is spying without the certainty of being betrayed by his physical appearance. But, in this respect, the Hallichek Ambassadress and her Embassy staff were sorely hampered. And the bugs planted by the avians—not very expert electronic engineers—were easily detected. Of course, there are—and always have been and always will be—members of every intelligent race who will sell anything to anybody as long as the price is high enough. However, all such paid agents of the Hallicheki were known to the President's secret police, and care was taken that they were kept well away from all sources of important information.

There was telepathy, of course, and there was at least one trained telepath at the Hallichek Embassy. Metzenther, working with a team of local biological engineers, had produced a number of personal thought-wave jammers, each of which consisted of a fragment of cat's brain, kept alive in a tiny vial of nutrient solution, which continuously broadcast on an emotional rather than an intellectual level, which screamed hungrily—and the hunger motivating the scream was for the red, bleeding flesh of birds, any sort of birds. Trafford, who liked cats, always felt unhappy when he slipped the little cylinder into his pocket. The jammers were not necessary in the environs of the spaceport, nor were they required in the Presidential palace—both these localities were literally infested with the animals, especially bred for their qualities as telepathic transmitters.

Meanwhile, there was misdirection. Now and again *Wanderer*'s people would make an appearance in the uniform of the Antrim Navy, which involved no more than a change of cap badge, buttons and shoulder boards. The token shipment of cargo, when it was loaded, was camouflaged as ship's stores. Painters slapped a coat of gray over the Terran insignia on *Wanderer*'s bows—a covering that could be sluiced off in seconds, with the correct chemical wash, just prior to lift-off.

The convoy conferences were held under conditions of strictest security. Nobody was present except the captains and specialist officers of the ships that would be sailing in company. There was Huetzen, commanding officer of one of the corvettes and flight master of the Kokreli merchant squadron. There were gunnery officers, communications officers, and engineers.

This Huetzen was an even more commanding figure than the Agent General. He was not so tall—was small by the standards of his race—but he made up for it by force of personality. Trafford had often heard undersized and aggressive humans referred to as "real fighting cocks," but this was a *real* fighting cock. He thought, *I'm glad he's on the same side as me.*

He felt oddly flattered that this gaudily plumaged being was treating him with respect, and relieved that the avian was willing to turn over to him the effective command of the convoy—and more relieved still that Irene refrained from harping on the legalities and illegalities of such a situation. Since his resignation from the Imperial Navy he had had his bellyful of Merchant Service red tape.

"It iss an honor," hissed the Flight Master, "to lift ship under your command, Captain. Your superb spacemanship vhen you evaded the blockade . . ."

"The credit goes to my Chief Officer and my Chief Engineer," said Trafford, embarrassed.

"So you say. But the Captain iss the leader. Vithout him, the ship iss no more than dead metal. But ve are grateful to you. Ve vished to lift ship months ago, to take our chance. But the Agent General—that old hen!—iss the ruling Kokrel authority on thiss vorld. His orders vere that ve remain. But now, vith your fire power . . ."

"The Agent General acts in the best interests of his government," pointed out Irene, unable to maintain silence for long. "After all, to throw away ships needlessly, uselessly . . ."

"But he iss a *civilian*, madam."

"So are we," she pointed out.

The Flight Master laughed discordantly. "You, civilians! With a ship that ve vould be proud to have in our Navy! But, vith your permission, to business. Little time is remaining. It iss essential that I and my officers understand vhat the Captain requires of us."

"This will be the last briefing," said Trafford. "We lift ship as a squadron. You, sir, as Flight Master, will lead in your *Quetzol*. We, in *Wanderer*, will be next in line astern of you, screened by *Sessati*, *Sitangi*, *Serramar*, and *Sekara*. Astern of us will be *Quetzang*. It is essential that our own ship shall remain hidden, as it were, with her national colors obscured, until the shooting starts. And then once we, the innocent neutral, are fired upon with neither warning nor provocation, we start shooting back."

Huetzen opened his beak wide in the Kokrel version of a laugh, his black tongue darting snakelike. He squawked, "You are cunning bastards, you Terrans. Ve have not your subtlety. But I can imagine how those upstart hens vill squawk vhen they find they have a poison lizard by the tail!

"And now. Vhen the action commences, you vill the orders give. That is correct?"

"That is correct, Flight Master. Unluckily we are short of linguists—only you can speak English and none of us has a command of your language—but the code that we have worked out should be more than adequate."

"It vill be. Already ve have rehearsed in the battle simulator lent to us by the Antrim Navy."

"Good."

There was a pause while Huetzen delivered a translation of what had so far been discussed with his officers, during which *Wanderer*'s people talked among themselves on the subject.

"And now, Captain, after our victorious action ve proceed in company. Yess?"

"Yes. I trust that all your engineer officers have made the necessary modifications so that their Drive governors may be tuned to our master synchronizer. We shall make the voyage under random precession, of course."

"Of course. Ve must remain in company. The hens have more ships than ve do, and their squadrons are flapping all over this sector. Ve may be attacked anyvhere." He added cheerfully, "I hope ve are."

"I hope we're not," Irene told him tartly. "Our ships—including your own, Flight Master—are cargo carriers. Our job is to carry a shipment of grain from Point A to Point B as expeditiously as possible. Should we be attacked, we shall defend ourselves to the best of our ability—but, whenever possible, we shall run rather than fight. I'd like that clearly understood, Flight Master."

Huetzen glared at her, then asked Trafford, "You allow this, Captain?"

Trafford said, "It's all rather complicated. I am her superior officer, but she is my employer."

"Ve have not such complications. On the Kokreli worlds, hens are never more than servants."

"And on the Hallicheki planets, that is the status of the cocks," said Irene.

"And that ve vill change."

"I'm not altogether sure," said Irene to Trafford, "that we

are on the right side in this squalid squabble."

"That's a matter of opinion, my dear. But since you love harping on legal technicalities, I'll point out that we have signed the Charter Party and are, therefore, bound to deliver the goods."

"I suppose we have to." She was on her feet now, confronting the avian, exchanging glare for glare. Hers was as flamboyant a personality as his was, and the only surprising thing about the clash, thought Trafford, was that it had not come before.

He stood up himself, intervened his body between those of his wife and the hissing bird, putting on, like a hastily assumed garment, his best quarter-deck manner. "Flight Master Huetzen!" he snapped. "Mrs. Trafford! That will be all. Unluckily, sir, as a neutral I can exercise no legal control over you, but I want it clearly understood that I, commanding the most heavily armed ship in the convoy, shall be giving the orders. And I want you to understand that too, Mrs. Trafford. Owner you may be, but you are not Master. Once we have lifted, you are bound to obey my lawful commands."

There was a tense silence, then Huetzen gave a short, clucking laugh. "That iss right, Captain. Tell her to go and lay an egg."

"And I'd like to convert *you* into southern fried chicken!"

"Stop that!" snapped Trafford.

"We haven't lifted ship yet," Irene snapped back. "As Owner, I can fire you. Here and now."

"Do you want a suit for illegal dismissal on your hands?" he asked her coldly.

She fell back into her chair, laughing. "You've been learning too well," she said at last. "You damned space-lawyer!"

"And now, Captain," asked Huetzen, "shall ve proceed with the conference?"

XVI

AND SO, AT LAST, the date and hour of departure were fixed. Convoy procedure, and the strategy and tactics to be employed in the all too likely event of enemy action, presented no real problems—but the frequent clashes of personalities, interracial and intraracial—did. Some of the Kokreli captains resented having to take orders from an alien, a mammalian alien at that. And Irene did not like being obliged to take a back seat.

Lift-off day dawned fine and clear. Trafford looked up from the control room viewports to the cloudless sky, to the pale blue ceiling above which the warships of the Hallicheki maintained their ceaseless patrol. It seemed to him that countless beady eyes were peering down at the green world of Antrim, that the early birds were alert to catch the juicy worms that would soon be emerging from their burrows. *But these,* he told himself, *would be worms with claws and teeth,* and felt a little happier.

He turned his regard from the menacing sky to his more immediate surroundings. He saw that the dockyard painters had removed the disguising coating from the Terran insignia on *Wanderer's* hull plating. At the far end of the field he could see the six Kokreli ships. At the sharp prow of one of them, the corvette *Quetzol,* a brilliant red light was blinking. But the transceiver, save for a faint hiss and crackle of interference, was silent. The port authorities had agreed to waive the usual departure procedure, and, as far as possible, everything was to be done by visual signals.

One by one, on the bows of the other ships, the prepatory blinkers flashed into life. At a nod from Trafford, Susanna switched on the light at *Wanderer*'s stem. It was reflected ruddily from the glass and the polished metal of the control instruments, and brought an odd, flickering flush to the set faces of the people sitting tensely in their chairs. Only Irene seemed at ease, conveying the impression of a superb, unself-conscious self-confidence.

She said, "Very soon the balloon will go up."

Trafford grunted acknowledgement. His attention was focused on the signal lamp at the flagship's prow. Suddenly it went out—the executive—and, a split second later, the other lights were switched off. Almost imperceptibly, *Quetzol* lifted, hanging for long seconds a scant few inches above the concrete. An eddy of dust swirled under the venturi of her silent emergency rockets, around the wide vanes of her tripod landing gear. And then she was rising faster and faster, and *Sessati, Sitangi, Serramar* and *Sekara,* the four fat merchantmen, were off the ground, as though jerked into the air by a single string.

Quetzol was little more than a black speck against the sky, and below her the cargo vessels were maintaining a beautifully spaced pattern when Trafford, watching the clock and acting upon the information relayed to him by Susanna at *Wanderer*'s radar, put his own inertial drive into operation. Once well clear of the spaceport buildings he applied lateral thrust until the other ships were directly overhead, and then increased speed so as to bring *Wanderer* into station. While he was so doing he heard the report that *Quetzang* was off the ground and following astern.

At the touch of a button the armor screens slid up over the viewports. The convoy was not yet clear of the atmosphere, was still in territorial space, but it would not do to assume that the Hallicheki would be overly fussy about legalities. Tallentire, at his control panel, was ready—as, no doubt, were the Kokreli gunners at their own consoles.

Irene said, breaking the silence, "Susanna, is the recorder ready?"

"Yes, ma'am."

"Good. Then, before any shooting starts, I'd like to make a record. Switch on."

There was a faint click.

"I, Irene Trafford, née Irene Smith, am the registered owner of the cargo vessel *Wanderer*. The ship's defensive armament is my own personal property. I hereby give permission to my employees—the Master and his officers—to use this armament as they see fit in the defense both of the ship and of their own persons in the event of illegal attack. That is all."

"Permission acknowledged," grunted Trafford, intent on his controls. Then, speaking with greater clarity, "I, Benjamin Trafford, Master of the cargo vessel *Wanderer*, acknowledge receipt of the instructions given me by the owner of said vessel. That is all."

"Switch off," ordered Irene.

Tallentire muttered something about seeing his solicitor before he pushed so much as a single button. Susanna told him, sharply, to shut up.

Even with the armor plating in position Trafford could still see an overall picture of the convoy, a better one, perhaps, than with the ports unobscured. All six Kokreli ships showed clearly on the viewscreens, as did the great globe of Antrim right astern. It was diminishing slowly but perceptibly, the curvature of the horizon already apparent. And now, visible only as tiny specks of light on the radar screen, were the first of the Hallicheki cruisers, the vessels of the orbital blockade, hastening to intercept and to destroy. With *Wanderer* screened as she was, the convoy would register on their instruments as a group of six ships—and six ships could be nothing but a Kokreli break-out.

Steadily the convoy lifted. Any attempt at evasion, before the bringing into operation of Interstellar Drive, would be futile. Maximum speed had been ordered by the Flight Master, and maximum speed, insofar as it was compatible with station keeping, would be maintained. Steadily the convoy lifted, through the last tenuous reaches of the atmosphere, a flight of metallic arrows aimed at the bull's-eye of the target that was forming itself out there in space, the great circle that was rimmed by at least twenty warships.

"They are ready for us," whispered Metzenther.

"A blinding glimpse of the obvious!" snapped Irene. Then in a softer voice, "By 'us' do you mean the convoy as a whole, or ourselves?"

"The convoy as a whole," the telepath replied. "My impressions are of a mob of enraged hens pecking a cockerel to death. I do not think that they suspect *our* presence."

"Good."

"Red, green, red, from the Flight Master," reported Susanna. "That means, 'All armament in readiness.' "

"Acknowledge," said Trafford.

The convoy lifted. The ships were out of the atmosphere now. Soon, very soon, it would be safe to actuate the Mannschenn Drive units. But the Hallicheki were all around them now, out of effective lasar range but with missiles ready in their racks—or already launched.

"Red, red, red," announced Susanna. "Repel missile attack."

"Remember your orders, Mr. Tallentire," said Irene.

"I am remembering, ma'am. I hope that our Kokreli friends are remembering theirs."

"They will."

Huge flowers blossomed briefly on the black fields of night, evanescent chrysanthemums of blue incandescence, as the stabbing laser beams and the questing anti-missile missiles of the Kokreli found their marks. This was the crucial point. One of those missiles must find its way through the screening merchantmen, must directly menace *Wanderer*. Then, and then only, would she be entitled to use her own weapons.

"Make blue, white, blue," ordered Trafford.

The signal flashed on, was acknowledged, and then the executive was made. From the sterns of *Quetzal* and the four merchant vessels flared the exhausts of the emergency rocket drives. The five Kokreli ships leaped forward, leaving *Wanderer* exposed.

"*Now!*" snapped Irene.

"*Now!*" echoed Tallentire, happily. His hands were poised over his console, his eyes intent on his radar screen. One forefinger stabbed downwards, delicately, three times. In quick succession three glaring explosions bloomed on the vision screens, so close that they blotched out all view of the rest of the convoy.

Susanna was speaking into her microphone. "*Wanderer* to Antrim Aero-Space Control. We have been attacked without warning. We are obliged to defend ourselves."

"Mr. Tallentire," ordered Irene, "open fire."

Tallentire launched his first flight of missiles, the deadly remote-control rockets that had no homing devices of their own but were maneuvered by the human gunner, that were effective only if that gunner was, like Tallentire, a near genius in his own field. While his attention was thus fully occupied, the ship could defend herself, would automatically launch anti-missile missiles, stab out with her anti-missile laser. It would be an extravagant defense, but in the circumstances it was unavoidable.

The missiles were aimed at the Hallicheki flagship, and as they sped through the emptiness, each nose cone released a shower of tiny rockets which were little more than darts, but which filled the space ahead with a cloud of arrowheads that would riddle and destroy the enemy counter-missiles. Tallentire grunted with satisfaction as the explosions showed on his screen, then released from each of his vicious flock a cloud of reflective, anti-laser vapor. At the last moment the flight split up, those in the center still aimed for the original objective, those to the left and to the right diverted to the next ahead and the next astern from the flagship.

Not all of them got through, but Irene, stepping up the magnification of the vision screen, reported that the flagship had a gaping hole amidships and that the ship astern of her had lost her entire tail section.

The Kokreli were fighting, and fighting hard, but they had not the fire power of *Wanderer*, and without her would have been able to do little more than to put up a not very effective defense against the Hallicheki salvoes. The pattern of the battle should have been the old, tried and trusted one— cripple with long-range missiles, close in to finish off with laser. It should have been, but, so far, it had been only units of the superior force that had been crippled.

Even so, the Hallicheki still had the superiority of numbers. With the exception of *Wanderer*, the ships of the convoy did not have missiles to throw away. *Quetzol* and *Quetzang* were the only lightly armed corvettes, and the merchantmen were designed for the economical carriage of cargo, not an equivalent tonnage of lethal ironmongery. Already the fire of the Kokreli ships was slackening, already what had been, initially, a veritable cloud of missiles and anti-missiles had dwindled to a thin scatter of rockets, economically employed, one for one. Only *Wanderer* was still maintaining a full defensive barrage and, at the same time, keeping up a sustained attack upon the blockading cruisers.

Still the convoy was not clear of the inner Van Allen Belt, still the change-over to Interstellar Drive was not possible. And ahead, right ahead and closing fast, were three of the

Hallicheki ships. *Quetzon* was firing with all her forward bearing armament, but it was in her own defense only. She could deal, still, with the enemy weapons, but not with the enemy themselves.

Trafford grasped the situation. "Blue, white, blue!" he snapped, adding, "and I hope they see it!"

There was delay, a delay that seemed to stretch into minutes. And then the message was repeated by the signal lights at the Flight Master's stern. Trafford gave the executive, and immediately pressed the firing key for his emergency rocket drive. The sudden acceleration forced *Wanderer's* people back and down into the padding of their chairs. Ahead of them, *Quetzol* loomed large and larger in the vision screen. And then, suddenly, she shifted to one side as the Flight Master applied lateral thrust. *Wanderer* surged past her, and it seemed that little more than the thickness of a coat of paint separated the two vessels. *Wanderer's* forward laser projectors were already in action, a flight of her own missiles preceding her. A blue-white hell exploded before her as her weaponry dealt with the Hallicheki rockets already in flight, and the clatter of fragments upon her armored hull was deafening.

And then—still small on the forward screen, but expanding fast—directly in their path, were the Hallicheki ships. The situation could no longer be dealt with by the prearranged code of colored lights. Irene, without orders from Trafford, took over the transceiver. "*Wanderer* to *Quetzol*. Do you read me?"

"Loud and clear," came the answer in Huetzen's squawking voice.

"Cover our flanks, *Quetzol*. Everything we have is being brought to bear before the beam."

"Villco, *Wanderer*. Villco."

The ship trembled from a near miss, near enough for the billow of expanding, incandescent gases to shove her violently from her trajectory. Trafford did not bother to correct course; it would have made little or no difference to the outcome of the battle. He heard, as though from very far away, somebody saying, "*Sitangi's* had it. . . . No, she's still coming on. . ." And then, "They're out of control! They'll be into us!"

"Lateral thrust!" Irene was shouting. "Full lateral thrust!"

Trafford could see the doomed merchantman in the vision screen, saw her, flaring fire gushing from her ruptured sides, sweep past the corvette *Quetzol*. Had it not been for that near-miss *Wanderer* would have been well clear of her line of advance; as it was, she was directly in *Sitangi's* path. The Inertial Drive generators howled as they were accelerated to their full capacity. *Wanderer* staggered, her entire structure strained and creaking. And then *Sitangi* was alongside them, almost aboard them, filling the starboard vision screen. She was past them, and the backwash of her rocket exhausts brought a suffocating heat to the Earth ship's control room. Her emergency rockets were roaring unchecked, uncontrolled, pouring away tons of reaction mass that would have sufficed for a score of reaction drive landings, a dozen battle maneuvers. And, Trafford guessed, the governor of her inertial drive must be broken, and the generators whirling to inevitable destruction. But he did not need Metzenther to tell him that there was more than mere chance involved, that *Sitangi* and her handful of survivors were screaming to their finish under the full command of her Captain.

Without orders, Tallentire maintained a covering fire for the stricken ship, sending his missiles around her and ahead of her. The three Hallicheki cruisers were plastering her with everything they had but, stupidly, were not taking evasive action. She drove among them and then, with dreadful suddenness, she exploded—her power plant and every missile remaining in her magazines making of her a huge, enormously destructive bomb. The flare of her passing washed over the screens, blinding the onlookers. And when, seconds later, *Wanderer* drove through the area, there was nothing but wreckage—battered and twisted hull-sections and a few space-suited Hallicheki, looking like grotesque, winged dinosaurs in their armor, that flashed and burst as *Quetzol*'s laser bemas picked them off, one by one.

Trafford was sickened, but kept his attention on his instruments, signaled 'Stand By Mannschenn Drive,' to Bronheim. It would be safe enough now. "Make blue, red, blue," he said quietly to Susanna.

"They've acknowledged," she told him, after a second's lapse.

"Good. Execute."

And on the viewscreens the hard, bright stars became distorted spirals of pulsing luminosity, and *Wanderer*'s Mannschenn Drive unit keened with an eerie irregular note as she, with the surviving ships of the convoy, fell through space-time to the whim of random precession.

XVII

THE HALLICHEKI PURSUED, of course. Twelve cruisers, matching velocity to the nearest millimeter second, englobed the convoy. The could not achieve temporal synchronization, so were invisible, no more than ominous blotches of light in the screen of the Mass Proximity Indicator. But they were far from inaudible, keeping up a continual clucking and squawking on the Carlotti bands. Sometimes a linguist would address her threats directly to the Terrans, but for most of the time the Kokreli ships were the target for the never-ceasing volleys of abuse. Trafford, finding a frequency upon which he could talk, briefly, without interruption, asked Huetzen what was being said. The Flight Master cackled cheerfully, "They say that they vill caponize us." Then, a wistful note in his voice, "They outnumber us only two to one. Let us synchronize and fight."

"No." Trafford was firm. "This is a convoy of merchantmen, not a squadron of warships. We have already lost one vessel. . . ."

"But she took three Hallicheki cruisers with her."

Maybe she did, Trafford thought, but the odds against the convoy were too heavy. Too much ammunition had been expended during the break-through, and there were no store ships available to replenish what had been used. Of the six ships, only *Wanderer* still had sufficient missiles in her magazines to fight a sustained engagement. Fully half of the laser projectors mounted by the merchant vessels were now unserviceable, and owing to some incredible stupidity on somebody's part all the spares had been carried aboard *Sitangi*. And *Sitangi* was now no more than a dissipating cloud of radio-active particles floating somewhere in the orbit of Antrim.

But, sooner or later, the convoy must make a return, however brief, to the normal continuum. In the heat of the action there had been no time to line up the ships on the target star, the Karakella sun. Already they were light years off course. To cut the Drive in order to correct trajectory would present the Hallicheki with a golden opportunity.

So they plunged on, down the dark, twisted dimensions, falling further and further away from their objective. They plunged on, with no more control over their trajectory than hypothetical microscopic beings living in the interior of an artillery projectile. It was no consolation that the Hallicheki were similarly handicapped; they could afford to play a waiting game far better than could their outnumbered adversaries. In all probability, one of the pursuing vessels was a supply ship, her holds stacked with missiles and with spares and replacements for the other weapons.

But something had to be done, and done soon. The convoy was supposed to be bound for Karakella, not for the Andromeda nebula.

Trafford in the privacy of their quarters, talked matters over with Irene. "Damn it all," he said, "I wish I could see some way out of this impasse. I feel worse than I did when I was the Red Jeddak's prisoner, seated in that overheated room, listening to the wolves howling outside in the snow...."

"Wolves," she said.

"Wolves?"

"Yes. Wolves. Furry animals on four legs, now found only in zoological reserves, that used to hunt in packs...."

"It's a flock of vicious old hens that we have to deal with, not a wolf pack."

"Think of them as wolves, Benjamin. And try to remem-

ber the stories you read about wolves when you were a boy.
Think of the travelers, in their droshky or sled or whatever
the horse-drawn vehicle was, fleeing across the steppes, pursued by the ravenous pack. . . . And what did they do?"

"According to the old stories, when things got really tough
they'd throw one of their number out of the sled, hoping to
gain a little time while the wolves tore him to pieces. . . ."
He added virtuously, "But we couldn't do that."

"Couldn't we? Apart from anything else, Huetzen—who
can be quite stupidly belligerent—would welcome the opportunity of going down with all guns blazing and all the rest
of it."

"No," said Trafford firmly. *"No."*

"But my idea has its merits, you must admit."

"It has. But . . ." Making a ritual of it, he filled and lit his
pipe, his usual aid to cerebration. "H'm. I'd like to talk this
over with the Flight Master, without having to code and
decode. A telephonic conversation *en clair* is quite impossible in these circumstances. . . . Even with the scrambler
it's not safe. . . ."

"Yes," she agreed. "And *they* must have telepaths aboard
their ships."

"We're safe enough here. Our ravenous tom cat psionic
jammers are still in operation. Now . . . it *is* possible to board
another ship when both vessels' Mannschenn Drive units are
in operation. But there must be physical contact—a thin
cable with a magnetic clamp would do—and there must be
perfect synchronization. . . ."

"We have that now."

"We haven't. Not so long as we're running on random
precession rates, even though our governor is the master
and the Kokreli governors are the slaves. There's always that
time lag—infinitesimal, but there, nonetheless. It's laid down

in Regulations that boarding is not, repeat not, to be attempted in such circumstances."

"You were brought up, Benjamin, to pay far too much attention to Regulations. In the Merchant Service . . ."

"Yes, yes. I've heard it all before. In the Dog Star Line you made up the rules as you went along. But, my dear, in the Navy we had far more experience of sailing in company than you ever did in your rough and tough star tramps. Some regulations, I admit, are made to be broken—but any that concern themselves with the safety of personnel are better observed."

"All right, then. So what do you suggest?"

"This. The convoy will have to synchronize, at a steady rate of temporal precession, for a matter of minutes. All we can do is to hope that the Hallicheki will be taken napping, but for the time that it takes Huetzen and his aides to board *Wanderer* all weapons, defensive and offensive, must be in a state of readiness. We're in visual touch with our own ships, so we shall be able to use the signal lights for part of it. A coded message should suffice for the rest."

"And when Huetzen's here?"

"Then we discuss just who is going to be thrown to the wolves."

"But I thought that you were against the idea?"

"Only up to a point, Irene. Only up to a point."

The operation went through without a hitch.

On the screens the images of the Kokreli ships lost their insubstantiality, their haziness, hardened and clarified. *Quetzol* had dropped astern of station, was now a mere half-mile from *Wanderer*. From the Terran vessel a contact rocket, its "warhead" a powerful electromagnet, trailing its gleaming cable, was guided by Tallentire to its target, the plating just abaft the corvette's after-airlock door. The door opened, and three space-suited figures emerged, grotesque, as their armored wing cases flapped against the nothingness until their talons caught hold of the tin wire. Swiftly, the Kokreli pulled themselves, claw over claw, across the gap between the two ships. When they were in *Wanderer's* airlock, the cable was disengaged, and before the winch had begun to reel it in, Bronheim, in his engineroom, had reset his master governor for random precession. There was no indication that the Hallicheki had suspected anything. Metzenther later summed it up—"They've got to the stage where everybody is talking and nobody listening—not even telepathically."

The boarding party removed their suits in the airlock, then were taken by Susanna to *Wanderer's* wardroom. They were offered—and they accepted—refreshment. Although they were not mammalian, they were warm-blooded oxygen breathers and, as such, shared many human vices, although the ingestion of liquor by soaking lumps of hard sugar in it and then crunching these lumps with noisy enjoyment, seemed a little odd.

Then, "Ve appreciate your hospitality, Captain," said Huetzen, "but I hope that thiss business iss important. It iss a serious matter for a Flight Master to leave hiss command in time of war."

"It is so, Flight Master Huetzen. But there are matters that we must discuss—er—beak to beak," said Trafford. "You know, as well as we do, that we are getting nowhere fast. We *must* return to the normal continuum to correct trajectory. But how?"

"As I have already said. All veapons in a state of absolute readiness, and fight."

"We just haven't got the firepower. But we can create a diversion."

"Vhat do you mean, Captain?"

92

"To begin with, Flight Master, which of your ships are expendable?"

"None of them," replied the avian. Then, proudly, "All of them."

"You must try to be realistic, Huetzen. Look at it this way. Your two corvettes are here only to ensure the safe arrival of the cargo vessels. *They* are expendable."

"Now we're getting somewhere," said Irene.

"Ve are. Ve are getting to the stage vhen the names *Quetzol* and *Quetzang* vill be written in letters of gold in the annals of the Kokreli Navy. Gladly ve vill sacrifice ourselves for the safety of the convoy—and of yourselves."

"I'm not asking you to sacrifice yourselves. We've lost too many people already. But I am asking you to sacrifice one ship—and a few tons of cargo." He gestured towards the manifests that littered the table. "I know what your merchantmen are carrying as well as the grain shipment, and that plastic sheeting is going to be useful."

"You talk in riddles, Captain."

"I'm sorry. But, before we go any further, will it be possible to take off *Quetzang's* crew and accommodate them aboard your ship and the others?"

"It vill be possible. Ve shall be a little cramped, vith no room to stretch our vings, but it can be done."

"Another point. We were lucky this time when we synchronized to allow you to board. We may not be so lucky the next time. Have you any suggestions as to how the attention of the Hallichek telepaths and Mannschenn Drive technicians might be diverted?"

"Vhy, yes. There iss a song, a song that ve can broadcast on all the Carlotti frequencies. It iss our national song. It never fails to infuriate those old hens." His throat swelled under the gaudy plumage, the bright yellow beak opened wide, and from it issued a raucous screeching, not without rhythm but utterly discordant, insufferably arrogant—Chanti-cleer saluting the dawn.

"It infuriates *me*," commented Irene drily.

"But of course. You, too, are a hen."

"But not an old one," contributed Trafford hastily. "And now, after all preliminaries, let us get down to the real business of the meeting."

XVIII

HUETZEN AND his officers were transferred back to their own ship—and this time, overriding Trafford's protests, there was no cessation of random temporal precession, although physical contact was established again between the vessels.

"To hell with Empress's Regulations!" swore Irene. "After all, I signed the stupid things."

"But you aren't the Empress now," pointed out her husband.

"Perhaps I'm not. But I'm a spacewoman still, and a good one. I know that there are times when one has to take a calculated risk—and this is one of them. We caught the Hallicheki napping once, but that's no guarantee that we shall be able to do it a second time, and a third, and as many times as a transfer of equipment and personnel is necessary. The way *I* see it, as long as there's a physical connection there *must* be perfect synchronization."

"She iss right," agreed Huetzen.

"She is not," snapped Trafford.

Nonetheless, he agreed to try the experiment. With the others he sat in *Wanderer's* control room, looking out through the now unscreened viewports to the dimly gleaming spindle that was *Quetzol*, the hazy, insubstantial shape of the corvette. Tallentire, an annoyingly supercilious smile on his lean features, lounged at his console. *This is a job for a gunnery officer*, his manner seemed to imply, *not for a navigator*.

A bright spark against the blackness, the contact rocket moved across the gap between the ships. It reached *Quetzol* —and went through her as though she did not exist. Tallentire muttered something, actuated his winch controls, and reeled in. He kept the little missile hanging barely clear of

Quetzol's shell plating and then, playing by ear as he later put it, set up a random variation of the strength of the field of the electromagnet in the rocket's nose. Then, suddenly, there was contact. The outlines of the Kokreli ship became hard, sharp. Insofar as random temporal precession was concerned, the two ships were as one.

"Satisfied?" asked Irene coldly.

"Yes . . . But it shouldn't have worked."

"But it did. Should it be necessary, we shall be able to hook up with every ship in the convoy."

"And how can we fight an action if we're all trapped in the middle of a damn steel-wire cat's cradle? You have to admit that there's some sense to the Regulations."

"All right, there is. But the chances of the Hallicheki's being able to synchronize are extremely slim, and we all know it."

Then, after Huetzen and his aides were back aboard *Quetzol*, there was so much that still had to be worked out, so many messages that had to be coded and decoded and, when it was absolutely necessary, visits to be paid to the other ships, *Quetzang* in particular. With practice Tallentire became extremely proficient in establishing and maintaining physical contact, but, with all vessels running under Interstellar Drive, the necessary maneuvering was not easy; radar had to be treated with extreme distrust, and the Mass Proximity Indicator did not function with any great degree of accuracy.

But the psychological problems were even greater than the navigational and engineering ones. Deputy Flight Master Hrista, commanding officer of the *Quetzang*, was even more belligerent than his superior. It had been a blow to his pride that in the action off Antrim the master of a merchantman, the *Sitangi*, had fought his ship to a finish, taking three of the enemy with him, while *he*, captain of a warship of the

Kokreli Navy, had made his escape. He was not at all unwilling that *Quetzang* should be sacrificed for the common good—but he wanted, as all his crew wanted, the ship's personnel to be part of the sacrifice.

There was a stormy meeting in the Deputy Flight Master's cabin. Trafford, who was accompanied by Bronheim, stood well back as Huetzen and Hrista confronted each other, wings widespread, plumage standing on end, steel spurs clattering ominously on the metal deck. Their hissing, squawking speech would have been too fast to follow even if Trafford had known the language. It seemed, more than once, that verbal violence would be followed by physical violence. And then, while the other still glared at him defiantly, Huetzen turned to the Earthmen.

"He wantss to die," he hissed. "He must strike hiss blow for the Federation. The captain of *Sitangi* wass hiss brood brother, but he vass rejected by the Navy because he vass lacking in fighting spirit. And now . . ."

"Tell him," suggested Trafford, "that there is an old Earth proverb:

> *'He who fights and runs away*
> *Will live to fight some other day.'* "

"That iss the first time I have heard that," cackled the Flight Master. "But it iss a good one. I vill tell him."

More argument ensued, but less heated this time. And when finally it was over, Trafford and Bronheim were able to get ahead with their real business, the setting up of fully automatic controls to all the ship's machinery, including her weapons, together with other controls that would enable her to be operated from the bridge of *Wanderer*. *Quetzang's* own technicians worked with them—but sullenly, resentfully. It was obvious that they shared the viewpoint of their captain and considered that *Sitangi's* last fight had put them to shame.

But the task was completed, and then there were the visits of inspection to the three merchantmen. Their officers were far easier to deal with. Theirs was the mentality, conditioned by their service, which considered the safe and speedy delivery of cargos as being, after all, of far greater importance than honor and glory, and they were willing to consider any means which would help them to attain this end. They knew the risks that would be involved if they worked outside their ships and were told that it was essential that they remain in physical contact with the vessels, by means of their lifelines, at all times. But Trafford realized that it would be impossible to carry out the work required within even those roomy hulls. The manipulation of huge sheets of plastic, no matter how light and flimsy, required space, and plenty of it.

The work went on, and as it progressed, the flagship jammed all the Carlotti wavebands with a continuous recording of that infuriating—even to human ears—national song. The irritation it would engender would, Trafford hoped, prevent the Hallicheki telepaths from picking up even the faintest clue as to what was being prepared.

It was a trying period, with humans and Kokreli working around the clock. *Sekara* lost her first mate and two spacehands—they disregarded the orders that they were not to release themselves from their lifelines, and by so doing released themselves from the continuum, from the Here and Now. Witnesses reported that the space-suited bodies had flickered eerily and then gone out like candle flames in a gale. *Serramar* lost an engineer who, by some improbable feat of acrobatics, contrived to puncture his suit with the shears that he was using. And there was a slight case of mutiny in *Quetzang*—aboard which vessel tempers were somewhat frayed—resulting in the demise of the gunnery officer when the Deputy Flight Master used his spurs more in rage than in self-defense.

And the worst of it all was that the full effectiveness of the plan depended upon just one thing, surprise, and Huetzen suspected that one of the Kokreli naval codes had been broken by the Hallicheki. It was no more than a suspicion, although a strongly grounded one. If it were correct, then the probability that things would go as planned was most unlikely. If it were not correct, there was still a chance of pulling it off.

At last everything was ready. *Quetzang*'s crew had been transferred to *Quetzol* and the three merchantmen. Huetzen and the merchant skippers had their orders. *Wanderer*'s officers sat in their control room, watching in their screens the other ships of the convoy, the distant, hazy shapes of them, distorted and flickering. All connecting cables had been reeled in so there was, of course, no longer exactly accurate synchronization.

Irene looked at Trafford, raising her eyebrows. He nodded, then snapped to Susanna, "Now!"

She touched a switch. The colored-light signal blinked on, was repeated by *Quetzol*. She made the executive. Abruptly, in mid-note, that raucous recording was switched off. In its place a stuttering succession of dots and dashes issued from the speaker of the Carlotti transceiver—similar to Terran Morse, but oddly spaced and accented. Trafford knew what it was saying. He had composed the message. *Quetzang to Flight Master. Request permission to fall back to investigate group of ships in my vicinity, believed to be Eighth Experimental Squadron. Shall endeavor to establish communication.*

There was a pause, then another crackling signal, obviously from another transmitter, and with a different hand on the key. (But, Trafford knew, from the same ship.) *Flight Master to Quetzang. Drop back to establish contact. Request*

Flight Master of Eighth Experimental Squadron to stand by us while we correct trajectory.

Then, with an odd, querulous note, *Quetzang to Flight Master. I shall do my best. But it is hard to establish contact with an experimental ship.*

With an ominous snap, *Flight Master to Quetzang. Establish contact.*

More lantern signals flickered from the stubby mast at *Wanderer*'s bows, and Irene's hands played over the console that gave her control over *Quetzang*'s movements. And aboard the merchantmen the captains would be pushing buttons that set into motion the simple machinery which had been installed inside the huge plastic balloons, balloons made to resemble ships, but ships of slightly odd design. Like great, gleaming ghosts they detached themselves from their parent vessels, vanishing as they fell out of the temporal precession fields of the Mannschenn Drive units. But they were still visible in the screen of the Mass Proximity Indicator, although only as the very faintest of sparks.

Quetzang, her interstellar drive shut down, her inertial drive running in full reverse, was dropping astern fast, and the flimsy giants were following her, homing upon her.

"They've swallowed the bait," murmured Trafford, staring at the screen of the Mass Proximity Indicator. "They've swallowed the bait. Ten of them. Quick thinking on their part, even though it's wrong thinking. A ship of this mythical Experimental Squadron, with some sort of souped-up Drive, would be a far better prize than a convoy of grain carriers. . . ."

"Their M.D.'s are off," reported Irene.

"Good. Mr. Tallentire, do you think you could manage some long range harassment from *Quetzang*'s stern batteries?"

"Can do, sir." Tallentire's fingers played over the duplicated console. "A flight of homing missiles should keep them busy for a little while."

The screen of the Mass Proximity Indicator showed very little. There were the sparks of light that were ships, the fainter sparks that were the decoys, the almost invisible scintillations that were flights of missiles. Tallentire could do very little now. He turned the control of *Quetzang*'s armament to her own fire control system, to the mechanical reflexes that would keep her fighting brainlessly as long as there was a missile in the racks, a circuit unbroken. And Trafford switched over to the corvette's auto-pilot, the device that had been so modified that it would throw the unmanned ship into a series of utterly random maneuvers, using both inertial and interstellar drives.

As for the decoys, they would play their parts. A direct hit with a laser beam or a missile would destroy them—but this destruction would leave no debris to register on the screens of either radar or Mass Proximity Indicator. And this, he hoped, would be a sore puzzle to the Hallicheki. A ship that disappears without trace, seemingly at will, must have something exceptional in the way of equipment. The Eighth Experimental Squadron might not be very good at fighting—but at running away, it would seem to be without peer.

Quetzang and the decoys could go through the motions of looking after themselves, but Trafford had to look after his remaining charges. "Mr. Metzenther," he asked, "how is it working out?"

"Fine, Captain. The hungry hens and the disappearing worms. And *Quetzang*'s doing quite nicely. That random firing pattern has them baffled."

"Good. Stand by for trajectory correction. And stand by all weapons, in all ships."

Susanna punched out the light signals.

XIX

As ONE SIHP, on the making of the executive, the convoy dropped back into the normal continuum. In the vision screens the hazy nebulosities, the distorted, pulsing spirals, were replaced by hard, bright stars. Astern, a long way astern, well out of effective range, was an unsteady coruscation, bright even though distant, where the doomed, unmanned *Quetzang* was still fighting, was somehow surviving because of the utter unpredictability of her actions. And there, too, the Hallicheki technicians must be flapping frantically over their instruments, trying to solve the mystery of the disappearing Eighth Experimental Squadron. But it would not be long before the Flight Marshal decided that a bird in the hand was worth two in the bush, before her cruisers came roaring back to dispose of the convoy.

The correction of trajectory could not be hurried.

Gyroscopes whined and the ships turned slowly about the spinning, universally mounted flywheels, hunting for the yellow spark, one of myriads of such sparks, that was the Karakella sun. Navigators, shutting their minds to the dangers outside the metal shells in which they worked, concentrated on the scintillating displays in their chart tanks, the gleaming filaments that were extrapolated trajectories. Communications officers listened intently for any telltale squawking and clucking from the speakers of their transceivers. Gunnery officers and spotters waited intently for any indication that the two remaining cruisers were returning to undistorted space-time, or that the main body of the fleet was giving up its futile search for the ghost ships.

Irene, as the most skilled navigator, was handling *Wanderer,* conning the ship, while Trafford swung her to his wife's orders. Tallentire, of course, was sitting hunched over his console, aching for the opportunity to use his weapons. Susanna was maintaining an overall watch on the detection and communications gear, while Metzenther, his face dreamy and oddly relaxed, was endeavoring to probe the minds of the Hallicheki.

He muttered, "Stand by. . . . Stand by. . . . I think that the Flight Marshal has ordered the two ships with us to engage us, regardless of cost, until the main body can come up. . . ."

Even as he spoke, the two vessels winked into being. They were close, within effective laser range, and opened fire before the clouds of reflective gas could be released. But they were hasty, too hasty, panicky, and the only damage done by their beams was the lopping off of the tail fins of one of the merchantmen. And then the missiles were loosed, by both sides. The volume of space within which the ships were slowly turning became a hell of incandescent vapors through which the deadly robots coursed and hunted. Missile clashed with anti-missile, and the deadly steel darts released by Tallentire's self-defending rockets sought and found their victims unfailingly. The two Hallicheki ships were outnumbered, but they had ammunition to throw away. The Kokreli were behaving as though the resources of their magazines were unlimited—and Trafford knew, all too well, that they were not, that they had been depleted to supply *Quetzang* with the wherewithal to give a good account of herself. And Tallentire was firing as recklessly as were the avians.

But Irene went on working, methodically, without panic or haste, even when the expanding gases from near misses buffeted the ship violently. "One degree, three minutes, forty-five seconds north declination . . . Three degrees, seven minutes, seventeen seconds east . . ."

"Check," replied Trafford, at the gyroscope controls. He

considered, as he made the necessary adjustments, ordering Tallentire to reduce his rate of fire to conserve ammunition. But he did not want to interfere. He knew, as well as did the gunnery officer, that the only possible defense against a missile attack is the saturation of the enemy's field of fire with anti-missiles. And he knew that the Hallicheki's own anti-missiles could only be beaten down by an overwhelming concentration of rocketry.

"South twenty-three seconds . . . West fourteen seconds . . ."

"The main body has opened fire," announced Susanna.

And how many seconds have we before their rockets get here? Trafford asked himself. A glance at the vision screens had told him that the merchantmen were now relying upon laser alone for their protection, and that *Quetzol* had only one battery in operation. Tallentire's fire was having to cover all six ships of the convoy, and could do so only as long as there were only two enemy vessels to contend with.

"North five seconds . . . East three seconds . . ."

"Check."

"Ready lights displayed by the merchantmen," announced Susanna.

"Steady, steady. Lock on at that."

"Locked on. Make the *Ready* signal, Susanna."

"Aye, aye. *Quetzol* reports readiness."

"Execute!"

And then, just as the convoy slipped back into the distorted continuum induced and maintained by its massed temporal precession fields, one of the Hallicheki cruisers blew up. *Wanderer's* vision screens blazed with blinding light, then went dead, burned out. But it didn't matter. The necessary repairs would occupy only hours and, owing to the initial deviation, the voyage to Karakella would take weeks of subjective time. And it was safe, now, to withdraw the armor from the viewports.

Yes, they were all there—*Quetzol* and the three cargo carriers, scarred and battered, but in perfect station. And the Hallicheki were there too—but only as distant sparks in the screen of the Mass Proximity Indicator. They could never catch up now, although there was the possibility that they might have another squadron hanging in orbit off Karakella. But that was doubtful. The planet would have its own defenses—ground-based and mounted in armed and armored satellites—as well as units of the Kokreli Navy within call.

Huetzen's voice cackled triumphantly from the speaker of the transceiver. "Now ve go as the crow flies—straight home. I have ordered the joining together of the two parts of the master stay. Vill you join us?"

Trafford's eyebrows lifted in puzzlement as he looked enquiringly at Irene. She shrugged her own bewilderment. Metzenther smiled slightly, saying, "It is bad form to eavesdrop on the mind of an ally, but sometimes necessary. He means that he has ordered all hands to splice the mainbrace."

"Then make it so," said Trafford to Susanna.

As the girl left to fetch bottles and glasses the telepath remarked, "That's one thing that I like about these Kokreli—their psychology is not too alien to ours. But those squawking old hens seem to possess none of the minor, pleasant vices, although they have all the minor, unpleasant ones."

XX

THE CONVOY SPED ONWARD and, directly ahead, the Karakella sun began to assume the appearance of a spiral nebula, a nebula whose arms were oddly twisted, a nebula that pulsed like a variable and shone with an ever-shifting play of rainbow colors. Astern, the Hallicheki squadron had given up the chase, but *Wanderer*'s sensitive Mass Proximity Indicator picked up what seemed to be no less than two considerable bodies of ships, one on the starboard beam, one on a relative bearing that was directly overhead. They were distant as yet, too distant to register on the Kokreli instruments, but the indications were that they were both steering converging courses. Irene ran up an extrapolation of all three trajectories in the chart tank, and, even with the scanty data available, it was obvious that they must intersect just off the world of destination.

And the strangers were ominously silent. There was no non-stop torrent of cackling from the Carlotti speaker. There was no reply to the signals made by *Wanderer*, although she was already in touch with the Karakella Flight Coordination. But Metzenther said, "They're Hallicheki, all right. I'm picking up the usual thought images of those inevitable birds of prey swooping upon fat pigeons. But . . ."

"But what?" asked Trafford.

"But the only ones I'm sure about are the ones out there. . . ." He waved a vague arm upwards. "I know it's far from reliable, but I can get a sort of directional fix. But the others . . . they're dead, dead, insofar as psionic radiation is concerned. I know that the Imperial Navy was playing around with various blanking effects, but have the Hallicheki anything of that kind?"

Trafford said that he didn't know, adding wrily that he supposed that the hens were entitled to their own experimental squadrons.

So it looked as though, after all, they would be intercepted. *Wanderer*'s inertial drive was not operating at full capacity, and she might be able to put on a burst of speed, to reach the protection of the planet's orbital forts before the enemy's arrival off Karakella. So might *Quetzol*. But the merchantmen were running flat out—and one of the axioms of naval warfare has always been that the speed of the convoy is the speed of the slowest ship. Huetzen would never dream of saving himself whilst leaving his charges to face certain destruction. *And neither*, thought Trafford, *can I.*

Flight Coordination was advised of the situation. Flight Coordination replied that it already knew. And Flight Coordination ordered—although, legally, it could only suggest —"Stand on."

"Tell those bird-brained bastards, 'Wish you were here,' " snapped Trafford irritably to Susanna. She coded the message, tapped it out. There reply came crackling back. Decoded, it read, "Not to worry. Stand on."

"They seem to possess a touching faith in our capabilities," said Trafford to Irene. "I suppose they expect us to pull a rabbit out of the hat, as we did off Antrim. But we can't. Not this time. *Quetzol* might manage it, but not the merchantmen."

"And why not?" she flared.

"All right, all right. Merchant officers are at least as good as naval officers. You've told me enough times. But they just haven't the gear to work with. Come to that, *Quetzol*'s navigational equipment is nothing like as good as ours."

"In any case," she told him, "it wouldn't work. Not a second time. Our feathered friends will be expecting a repetition of the maneuver and will englobe the entire planet with their ships. They'll be watching the back door as well as the front."

"So we stand on," he said.

"What else can we do? We aren't making any money by chasing all around the galaxy looking for a safe place to land. We stand on, and hope that we have enough anti-missile missiles in the racks to cover us until we're covered by the forts." She added, "I've already told Tallentire to convert all his rockets for defensive use only. He's sulking hard, but he's doing it."

Shortly afterwards, a conference was held aboard *Wanderer*, attended by Huetzen and the three merchant captains—all of whom possessed at least a slight command of English. None of the avians had heard of any device or technique by which psionic radiation could be blocked, although they admitted that the Hallicheki, the females of their race, were far more adept at the telepathic arts than themselves. Regarding armament, they were far more definite, although discouragingly so. *Quetzol* could loose off one full salvo, and that was all. The other three ships had five missiles between them, had less than half of their laser projectors serviceable, and, furthermore, had expended their last cylinders of anti-laser smoke-screen gas.

Huetzen was willing to attempt the maneuver that *Wanderer* had successfully employed when coming in to Antrim, but the merchant captains were far from enthusiastic. Their homes were on Karakella, and they knew what would happen on the surface of that world if anything went wrong.

The only ray of hope—although it was a feeble one—was provided by Huetzen. He said, "I know Flight Coordinator Hrazza. I know him vell. I served under him vhen he vas a Flight Master. He hass one great fault. Alwayss he iss too concerned vith safety."

"But it's not his safety that's involved," Irene pointed out.

"It's all very well for him to say 'Stand on' when he's not going to be shot at."

"He is a Kokreli!" snapped Huetzen. "His own safety to him iss less than nothing. But the safety of any ships under his command is all important."

"We aren't under his command," said Trafford.

"According to Kokreli spatial law you are," said the avian, "as long as you are in this convoy, chartered by our government."

"Could he have his own fleet standing by?" asked Irene. "It would have to be a big one, to be able to deal with at least forty ships on anything like equal terms."

"No. I do not think so. The Kokreli main fleet, according to the last reports I received, iss off Karahar, the very heart of the Federation."

"But you think this Flight Coordinator Hrazza knows what he's doing?" asked Trafford.

"I *know* that he knows vhat he is doing!" snapped the Flight Master. "If he orderss 'Stand on,' then he hass hiss reasons. And, Captain, I am a bird of honor. I vould not expect you to throw away your ship and your lives in a battle that iss not yourss. Ve shall bring thiss voyage to a successful conclusion. Of that I am certain!"

And with that *Wanderer's* people had to be content, and in the chart tanks the three gleaming filaments of the extrapolated trajectories converged upon the speck of light that was Karakella.

And still Trafford could see no solution to the problem. As soon as the convoy emerged into normal space it would be boxed in, would be obliterated by overwhelming fire. With as many as forty hostile ships in space the planet's orbital forts would be hard put to it to defend themselves, would be unable to contribute more than a token missile or two to the protection of the convoy. And it was now too late to consider an alteration of course, a heaving to for the purpose of setting a new trajectory. (But, in any case, to where?) A return to the normal continuum, however brief, would bring salvo after salvo of deadly missiles homing upon them. And, even had the materials been available, the "experimental squadron" ruse would not work a second time.

It was all very well for that Flight Coordinator on Karakella to say, "Stand on, stand on," but did he know what the convoy was up against? Could he know? Or—but this was only a faint hope—what did he know?

Stand on, stand on.

It seemed to *Wanderer's* people that the control room chronometer was ticking away the last hours of their lives. Fatalistically, they did the things that had to be done, filled the time with the minutiae of shipboard routine. Trafford was reminded of something he had once read in a historical novel, the proud tradition of the English Brigade of Guards —*They died with their boots clean.* If *Wanderer* was to die, she would die fighting, and she would die with every square centimeter of unpainted metal polished to mirror brightness. (Tallentire even burnished the castings of his missiles.) She would die with all her papers in order, with all loose ends neatly tucked in.

And now, with what must be the last voyage almost over, they were very close together—Trafford and Irene, Tallentire and Susanna. Trafford, as Master, officiated at the simple ceremony that made the Second Mate and the Purser man and wife. There was champagne, and there was a cake that Bronheim, displaying a hitherto unsuspected talent, baked for the occasion. It was, as Irene said, as corny as all hell, but corniness is not to be despised, and at times its manifestations have their uses.

As the point of impact of the three forces, that ominous

intersection of three glowing filaments in the chart .tank, grew closer and closer, life assumed an ever more dreamlike quality. For Irene and Trafford as well as for Tallentire and Susanna it was a honeymoon, and Bronheim and Metzenther were able to cope easily with the working of the automated ship, to maintain the watch on the various instruments.

It was Bronheim who hammered on the door of Trafford's cabin, waking him and Irene from a deep, peaceful sleep. He was oddly excited. "Captain," he said, "I hate to disturb you. But something funny is happening."

Irene, pulling the sheet up to her chin, remarked somewhat sourly, "Then make us laugh, Mr. Bronheim."

"I didn't mean it that way, ma'am. It's just that one of the enemy squadrons seems to be carrying out a very strange maneuver."

Abruptly, Trafford made the mental switch from the lover resentful at being disturbed to the conscientious captain. He knew Bronheim, and knew that this must be a matter of some importance. He jumped out of bed, hastily pulled on his uniform. He hurried after the engineer to the control room.

Bronheim gestured towards the Mass Proximity Indicator. "Look!"

Trafford looked. What he saw didn't make sense. It was obvious that the ships in the overhead relative position had made one of the slight alterarions of course that were possible with the Mannschenn Drive in operation, a deflection from the line of advance of only a few degrees, but sufficient to bring them across and through the track of the convoy. It was a futile, premature closing of the jaws of the nutcracker. Not that it would make any real difference. The Kokreli merchant squadron would still be exposed to terrible massed fire, although from one side only.

Susanna and Tallentire had been called, and they joined the others in the control room. The girl went to the communications equipment, and her husband to his fire control console. And Metzenther was there, wearing the dreamy expression that showed that he was concentrating hard. He muttered, "I'm getting something now. It seems to be the emanations that I associate with the Hallicheki, but somehow off-beat. Mechanical? No . . . But . . . phoney? Yes. That could be the word. The impression is that of a large bird of prey pushing a smaller bird of prey away from its victim—but I *feel* that the large bird should have fur, not feathers, and four legs instead of two legs and a pair of wings. . . . A tiger pretending to be an eagle? Hypnosis by telepathy? Could be. There's that blurred picture I keep getting of a hen being hypnotized by having its beak pushed down to a thick, black line on a sheet of white paper. . . ."

"But they *are* Hallicheki?" demanded Irene.

"They couldn't be anything else," said Trafford glumly. "If they were a Kokreli fleet they would have declared themselves before now. Those fighting cocks just don't believe in deception. No, it's just the old, old business, the same as we had off Antrim, of a squabble over the prize money, of two Flight Marshals, neither of whom will admit the right of the other to issue overriding orders." He turned to Susanna. "Get in touch with Huetzen, please. We'll see what he has to say about it."

The Carlotti frequencies were alive with squawkings and cacklings, so much so that the girl had to use code instead of telephony, punching the spaced dots and dashes of *Quetzol's* call sign through the avian screechings. And then, when at last contact was established, her query conditioned by the limitations of the Interstellar Code, she sent, "What are those ships?"

Meanwhile, the track of the convoy and that of the strange fleet had intersected. The screen of the Mass Proximity Indicator was ablaze with light. Temporal precession rates were not, of course, synchronized, so the crossing vessels, although briefly occupying the same position in space as the ships of the convoy, did not coincide in time. Even so, as Trafford had found during that unorthodox approach to Antrim, it was a tricky business. Outside the viewports huge, shadowy shapes were briefly glimpsed, and it seemed that *Wanderer* was threading her way through an incandescent web, the filaments of which were the strangers' trajectories, their luminous wakes through the continuum. Static crashed from the Carlotti speaker and pale St. Elmo's Fire danced and crackled on all metal surfaces. The hair of the two women stood out from their heads, glittering with tiny blue sparks. There was the acrid tang of ozone.

They were through and past, and the effects of the passage abruptly ceased. Radio communication was once again possible, and *Quetzol*'s reply stuttered from the speaker. Swiftly, Susanna jotted it down and then decoded. It was, "I do not know."

"Are they Kokreli?"

"Negative."

"Are they Hallicheki?"

"I do not know."

A strident squawk drowned even the stridulant code. This was, without doubt, a Hallicheki voice. It was speaking in English. "Flight Marshal Phryxic to *Vanderer*. Flight Marshal Phryxic to *Vanderer!* Surrender. Surrender. You are outnumbered. Surrender to *us*, ve vill peck the flesh from your bones!"

And a bored, supercilious voice broke in, "I'm afraid that's out of the question, old girl. Just run off somewhere, will you, and lay yourself a nice, fat egg."

"Who said that?" demanded Irene, glaring at the others in the control room.

"None of us," Trafford told her. But he thought that he recognized the accent.

"Calling *Wanderer*," went on the voice. "Suggest that you and your ships synchronize."

"A trap!" snapped Irene.

"I don't think so," replied Trafford. Then, to Susanna, "You heard what the man said. Make the signal, will you? We'll do it all from this ship, with the master governor."

XXI

Signal lights flicked on, were repeated, and then, with the making of the executive, the irregular, off-beat throbbing of *Wanderer*'s Mannschenn Drive Unit steadied to a thin, high monotone. The hazy outlines of the Kokreli ships hardened, sharpened. There was a lag of not more than a second, a brief interval of time during which Trafford wondered whether or not he had done the right thing. Suddenly, shockingly, the distorted, intricately convoluted images of the stars out to starboard were blotted out by tier after tier of running lights, by rank after rank of gleaming hulls. By stepping up the resolution of the viewscreen Trafford could make out details of the individual ships—destroyers, cruisers and the mighty deadnaughts themselves. He could see, bright on the shell plating of the nearer ones, the insignia of the Imperial Navy—the winged, crowned globe superimposed upon a stylized lightning flash.

And among them—dwarfed, outnumbered—were the other warships, the cruisers upon whose sides the stooping hawk stood out in bright-gleaming neon. And there was the avian voice squawking from the Carlotti speaker, "Vhat is this? Vhat is this? This is piracy!"

"This is my intervention," replied the bored voice. "This is intervention, old girl—and, may I add, long overdue."

"Ve protest! Ve protest!"

"Protest all you like, but do not, repeat not, attempt to molest the Kokreli convoy. We have . . . er . . . taken it under our wing."

"Ve shall lodge a complaint with your Empress!"

"Do just that. Meanwhile, sheer off. Or, if you prefer

stronger language, get the hell out of here. Any attempt to hamper our maneuvers will be severely dealt with."

There was a silence for a while as the Hallicheki squadron pulled itself clear of the Terran fleet. "It seems," admitted Irene reluctantly, "that what used to be *my* Navy has its uses. But I still can't understand how they pulled off that piece of deception, how they were able to fool the Hallicheki until the last moment. . . ."

"I think I know how it was done, ma'am," Metzenther told her. "Before I left the Service I had heard of a new training course for Psionic Communications Officers. Essentially, it was concerned with the techniques of telepathic hypnotism, the induction of hallucinations in the minds of other telepaths. This technique must have been in use. That was why the Imperial Navy ships were telepathically dead for so much of the time, as far as I was concerned. The psionic personnel were concentrating on the Hallicheki. . . ." He added, "The technique seems to work."

"I'll say." Irene lit a cigarette, looked through the wreathing smoke at her husband. "And now what, ex-Commander Trafford? Your precious Navy has saved our skins, but is it merely so that we may be tried for our crimes in a Terran court? Shall we be up before the beak as pirates, or as *franc tireurs*? I seem to recall that during the first of the World Wars that was the crime of which a certain Captain Fryatt was accused by the Germans. They shot him. Has the sheriff saved us from the lynch mob only so that he may have the pleasure of adjusting the hemp necktie about our necks?"

"But I thought," complained Trafford, "that we were legally in the right in everything we did."

"I think that we are, too." She permitted herself a half smile. "But once matters get into the claws of the legal eagles, who can tell what the final outcome will be? Even now, some genius might come up with some precedent about which we have never heard which could easily result in our being pushed out of our own airlock without space suits. . . ."

"You're damn cheerful," Trafford told her.

"Realistic, my dear. Realistic."

The Carlotti speaker came alive again. *"Inflexible to Wanderer. Inflexible to Wanderer.* Request that you and the ships under your command take up stations as allocated, proceeding to your destination. We shall escort you in."

Trafford took the microphone handed to him by Susanna. "Thank you, Admiral Cook-Willoughby. We shall do as you request."

The Admiral chuckled tolerantly. "You'd damn well better, young Trafford. It's high time you stopped playing at pirates and started being a good boy. Any trouble from *you,* and we'll treat you the same as we would the Hallicheki."

"We shall cooperate, sir." Then, rather nastily, "We have no option." Trafford infused warmth into his voice. "But I must say that we were surprised, very pleasantly surprised, when you came on the scene. May I ask you how it happened?"

"You may *not.*" Again the tolerant chuckle. "Matters of high policy do not concern relatively junior naval officers, especially when they are *ex-*naval officers. Just thank your lucky stars that we happened along. Oh, by the way, you might see to it that your wardroom bar is well stocked with mother's ruin and Angostura bitters. You owe me at least six pink gins."

"It will be a pleasure to drink with you again, sir."

"I shall enjoy the gins—and a talk," promised the Admiral. "Over and standing by on Channel 14Z."

"Over and standing by, sir."

Irene regarded Trafford quizzically. "So your buddy's not going to have us hanged from the yardarm after all, not even with our old school ties. That's one small comfort, even though he will drink us out of house and home." She levered herself out of her acceleration chair. "Well, Captain Trafford, she's all yours. Everything's over, including the shooting. The Hallicheki are outgunned and outnumbered and, if the Mass Proximity Indicator is to be believed, they're already in full flight for some other neck of the woods. So—with your permission, Captain, sir—I shall resume my broken slumbers."

"I wish I could join you," said Trafford sincerely. But he knew that he would not be able to do so. There was so much to do now. There would be the tedious business of fitting the Kokreli convoy into the Imperial Fleet. There would be the endless flow of signals from ship to ship, and between himself, Huetzen, the Admiral and the Flight Coordinator on Karakella. There would be coding and decoding. There could be—although this was extremely unlikely—some sort of desperate cutting-out operation on the part of the Hallicheki.

But the period of vigilance, of watch on and stay on, would not be a long one.

Within hours the convoy would be dropping down to the serenity of Port Karakel.

XXII

THIS WAS Karakella, journey's end until the commencement
of the next voyage, a windy world, the katabatic gales sweeping down from the sharp-peaked, snow-capped mountains,
driving airborne torrents of golden leaves and crimson wind-
flower blossoms through the narrow streets of the cities.
Her proud people rode the storms on wide-stretched wings,
disdaining mechanical aids, shrieking their defiance to the
forces of nature.

This was Pork Karakel, a small city in area but with its
buildings towering high into the turbulent sky, steeples of
masonry and metal latticework, each topped with a weather
vane wrought to the semblance of a crowing cock. It was
set on a hill top, buffeted by every wind, washed clean by the
racing air currents that brought with them the tang of the
snows of high places, that scoured the apron of every speck
of debris, that were bitterly cold but invigorating—veritable
elixir after the stale, cycled, and recycled atmosphere of the
ships.

It was a wild, romantic frontier world but, nonetheless,
one on which all the formalities concerning the movements
of merchant shipping had still to be observed, one on which
full reports of the conduct of the convoy had to be made,
both verbally and in writing, to the authorities.

There was Flight Coordinator Hrazza, gaudier, more flamboyant by far than any of the Kokreli Trafford had so far
encountered. Huetzen had insinuated that his superior officer was something of an old hen, but Trafford did not find
him so. His concern for the safety and well-being of any
vessels under his command was fiercely paternal rather than
maternal. And he hated the female sex; it was all too obvi-

ous that he was having to force himself to be polite to Irene and Susanna, that he was taken aback that a ship that had performed so valiantly numbered women among her crew, and one of those women in a position of importance.

There was the Port Master, Military, who was concerned with the replenishment of *Wanderer*'s magazines. Tallentire was impressed. "It was never like this in our Navy," he said. "There I had to fight for as much as a single missile over and above establishment. Here, anything and everything I ask for is forthcoming at once."

Irene said, "I hope their taxpayers can afford it."

There was the Port Master, Engineering, with whom Bronheim worked. He, too, was satisfied. "A bird he may be," he admitted, "but he's not bird-brained."

There was the Port Master, Stevedoring, with whom Irene clashed. There were all too frequent screaming matches over the discharge of the few tons of grain that *Wanderer* had carried. Finally, Trafford had to take charge while his wife sulked in her quarters. All that he wanted to do was to get that handful of sacks out of the ship, as soon as possible, and it did not matter to him if *Wanderer*'s own gear was employed, or the conveyor belts and gantries belonging to the port. Then it was his turn to sulk when Irene upbraided him bitterly for not having noted and registered a protest regarding the few small items of stevedore's damage.

Then dropping down from the flagship, came Willoughby-Cook in his Admiral's Barge. *Inflexible*—a màssive hulk, practically a powered orbital fort—could not land herself, was hanging in orbit with the rest of the fleet. Trafford and Irene almost came to blows again. He wanted to receive the Admiral with full naval honors, and she told him that even recorded bo's'ns' pipes were out. "You," she said, "are skipper of a tramp. In many respects your powers exceed those of a mere admiral. You—if I may use an archaic phrase—are

Master under God. The Admiral is Officer Commanding the Ninth Fleet, answerable to the Lord Commissioners of the Terran Admiralty. I know that neither of us is religious, but, even so, I think that the Almighty ranks somewhat higher than even the top brass of the Imperial Navy."

So there was no piping aboard, although Trafford and his officers, washed behind the ears and in their best uniforms, stood to attention just inside the main airlock as the tall, slim Willoughby-Cook strode up the ramp. The Admiral smiled slightly as he looked at them. He said, "You keep a taut ship, Captain."

"I do my best, sir."

"But of course, Trafford, the effects of naval training are hard to shake off, aren't they?"

"I, sir," said Irene coldly, "was never in the Imperial Navy."

"Weren't you, *ma'am?* I seem to remember a portrait of you, or somebody like you, all dressed up as an Admiral of the Fleet. . . ."

Hastily, Trafford took over, escorting the Admiral and his staff to the wardroom. Susanna was in charge of the bar and, already briefed by Trafford, served the Admiral with pink gins of triple strength. One effect of the liquor was to make the officer talkative.

"You know," he said, regarding his hosts over the rim of his glass, "you people were lucky, damned lucky. You were damned ingenious too, I admit that, both regarding your spacemanship and your handling of legal quibbles. I rather doubt, though, that your claim that a neutral merchantman can throw her weight around like a battle cruiser would hold water. . . ."

"There was a perfectly good precedent, Admiral," Irene told him.

"Perfectly good only if you happen to be on the winning

side. Thanks to the intervention of the Ninth Fleet you are on the winning side."

"And whom," she asked, "have we to thank for this intervention?"

"I'm sorry, ma'am. I'm not allowed to tell you. After all, matters of high Imperial policy are somewhat outside the ambit of even senior officers of merchantmen, even those who at one time held the exalted rank of Mate in the Dog Star Line."

"And so every snotty-nosed ensign in your Ninth Fleet knows . . ."

"They know nothing, ma'am," he said sharply. "All that my officers—apart from these gentlemen here, and they'll not talk—know is that the merchantman *Wanderer*, sailing in a Kokreli convoy from Antrim to Karakella, was being chivied by units of the Hallicheki Navy. They know that I was ordered to afford *Wanderer*, and the other vessels with her, full protection. That is all."

"Surely," said Trafford, "this must have excited *some* interest. . . ."

"Naturally, Captain. But you must recall from your own days in the Service the resentment that was building up over the maltreatment of Terran nationals by various aliens, the Hallicheki among them. And your reading of history will tell you that intervention is always legally justifiable if you can get away with it successfully."

"Anyhow," Trafford told him, "thank you, sir."

"Don't thank me, young Trafford. And don't thank the Lord Commissioners. Although I, personally, was very pleased to have been of service."

"I don't like all this secrecy," complained Irene.

"I'm sorry, ma'am, but that's the way it has to be. Orders is orders. Theirs not to reason why, theirs but to do and die, and all that. Volunteer for nothing and do as you're told."

The pale blue eyes that looked at her tolerantly had become a trifle bloodshot. "You know, ma'am, a year in Your—sorry, *Her*—Imperial Highness's Navy would do you a world of good. . . ."

"Careful, sir," admonished Trafford. "If you aren't careful, she'll be telling us all about the way they did things in the Dog Star Line."

"In the Dog Star Line," she muttered, "we didn't slink around hugging Dreadful Secrets to our bosoms." Then, in a louder voice, "What *is* behind all this?"

"It's a secret," replied Willoughby-Cook, poker-faced.

And that was all that he would tell them.

Finally, he and his aides made their departure, walking a little unsteadily across the apron to the waiting barge. Trafford and Irene, standing in the airlock, watched the guests leave. And then Trafford, noticing somebody else approaching his ship, stiffened. It was another human, an oddly familiar figure clad in drab gray that was all the drabber by contrast with the gaudy plumage of the port officials who accompanied him. Trafford had seen him before, in similar circumstances, had seen him standing in the middle of another group of aliens—although, on that occasion his coverall had been no more dowdy than the gray-green scales of the beings surrounding him.

"No," murmured Trafford. "It can't be. . . ."

"What?" demanded Irene.

"Look," he told her.

"You're right," she said. "It can't be. Not here. That must be one of the consular staff. After all, there must be more than one extraordinarily ordinary looking man in the galaxy."

"It can't be," said Trafford again. Then, as the man approached nearer, "But it is."

Smith held a brief conversation with the Kokreli who had walked with him to the ship, then marched up the ramp to the airlock. He said cheerfully, "It's a small galaxy, isn't it?"

"Yes, isn't it?" said Irene.

"Glad to have you aboard, Mr. Smith," said Trafford formally, shaking hands with the visitor. "Let me take you to the wardroom."

"Thank you, Captain. I could use an Earth-type drink. Frankly, I'm rather tired of the eggnogs that our hosts insist on serving. I know that the mixture has a certain ritual significance, but I find it all slightly disgusting."

"The eggs they use are not the eggs of their own kind," Irene told him.

"Yes, ma'am. But still *bird's* eggs."

"Don't be so damn silly. We're mammals, but we don't turn up our noses at the young of other mammals—lamb, or veal, or sucking pig—properly cooked and served. Anyhow, I think we can spare you a gin, if the Admiral's left any."

When they were all seated, with glasses in their hands, Smith said, "I was expecting to renew our acquaintance here, on Karakella. Or, perhaps, 'hoping' might be a better word. Shall we say that I foresaw this reunion through a glass, darkly?"

"Oh, yes," said Irene. "GLASS." Her manner thawed a little. "I hope that your people were pleased with the way that we carried out our first assignment, the shipment of antibiotics to Antrim."

"More than pleased, Mrs. Trafford. But that voyage to Antrim was only part of your first assignment. Much as the Galactic League for the Abolition of Suppression and Slavery wanted that shipment to go through, we wanted other things more. The . . . ah . . . fringe benefits. . . ."
bluntly.

"What the hell are you talking about?" demanded Irene bluntly.

"Let me put you in the picture. We knew that Flight

Master Huetzen and his ships were on Antrim, bottled up by the Hallicheki blockade. We knew that the Flight Master, given even only a slight chance of success, would attempt a break-out. You, Mrs. Trafford, provided that chance, as we thought that you would."

"Go on, Mr. Smith."

"From my reading of your character, we guessed that you would use the Kokreli ships to further your ends, just as the Kokreli used you to further theirs. And we were reasonably certain that an intelligent woman, especially one with your background, would figure out a way to bend Interstellar Law without actually breaking it. Which you, of course, did."

"Thank you, Mr. Smith."

The man leaned back in his chair, pointedly playing with his empty tumbler. Despite a warning glare from Irene, Trafford refilled it. Smith sipped with obvious enjoyment before resuming. "Finally, as we of GLASS hoped, you were the catalyst."

"The catalyst?"

"Yes. If I may be permitted a pun, we put the catalyst among the pigeons. Oh, you played a small part in affairs yourselves—thanks to you, a relatively unimportant convoy got through and the Hallicheki suffered minor losses. But you set a train of far more important events in motion.

"We, of GLASS, have long been dissatisfied with the state of affairs in this sector of the galaxy. There has been the Antrim business, of course. Confrontation is unpleasant and dishonest bullying that all too easily can blow up into open warfare—and, until now, the Antrimmers have been standing alone. We all know that they would not have stood the chance of a celluloid cat in hell if the Hallicheki had decided to be provoked into initiating actual hostilities. Insofar as the civil war is concerned, the one between the Kokreli Federation and the Hegemony, the stand of GLASS has been one of qualified neutrality. Qualified, I say, because the Kok-reli have always shown some respect for Interstellar Law and the rights of other races, whereas the Hallicheki work on the principle that whatever they can get away with is quite legal. There have been far too many innocent merchant vessels seized and their crews brutally maltreated for *our* liking.

"But what did the Imperial Government do about it? I'll tell you—although you, Mrs. Trafford, must already know. Just an occasional, politely worded note of protest. That was all.

"So . . ."

"So what, Mr. Smith?" Irene asked him coldly.

"So we decided to nudge the Grand Fleet into action."

"Did you, now? Do you mean to tell me that your subversive organization has infiltrated the ranks of the Armed Forces of the Imperium?"

Smith smiled sweetly. "You seem to forget, ma'am, that you yourself are no more than a mercenary employed by that same subversive organization. Although, I admit, you're a very special kind of mercenary. . . ."

"Go on."

"Putting it bluntly, ma'am, we know who you are—and what you were. Oh, the Empress Irene is back on Earth by this time, sitting on her throne, affixing her autograph to official papers and meddling in affairs of state as much as the Committee will let her—which won't be much. But who is fooled?"

"I don't know what you're talking about," Irene told him.

"Don't you? And neither, I suppose, does Captain Trafford. And to the other ex-commanders of the Imperial Navy, and to the ex-Lady Susanna, you're just plain Irene Smith, or Irene Trafford, owner of a merchant vessel that just happens to be a modified and more than somewhat improved light cruiser. I've no doubt that to the generality of the people of the galaxy the current Empress Irene is *the* Empress Irene—but, democracy notwithstanding, the generality of the people don't know, never will know and never can know as much as the high brass. The Lord Commissioners of the Admiralty know. Perhaps, just perhaps, Admiral Willoughby-Cook does not *know*, but he will have guessed.

"And most important of all, GLASS knows. And GLASS dropped a few hints in the right places. You can guess the way it was done. A highly popular ex-Empress who abdicated for reasons of the heart is, thanks to having acted in a public-spirited manner, in a most unpleasant jam. And what, if anything, is being done about it? Then, to make our case stronger, we had a few authentic photographs—borrowed, I may add, from Imperial Navy files—of human victims of Hallichek atrocities. That favorite threat of theirs, about pecking the flesh from prisoners' bones, is, I assure you, to be taken quite seriously. Our line of approach was this: *Do* something, or we spill the beans.

"So, finally, thanks to you we achieved a great deal. We jockeyed the Imperial Government into a position of what they call counter-confrontation. As and from now on, Terran ships are safe in this sector of the galaxy."

"Just a cat's paw, that's me . . ." muttered Irene.

"A cat's paw with claws," Smith assured her. "Furthermore, we now have absolute confidence in you and your ship."

"Thank you, Mr. Smith." Her manner brightened. "You've told us that the voyage from Antrim to Karakella was all part of GLASS's devious scheme to bring matters to a head. Well and good. But you chartered us only for the voyage from Slithlia to Antrim. It seems to me that we're entitled to hire for the Antrim-Karakella trip."

"You're a good space-lawyer," Smith told her, "but not good enough to talk me into that. It may interest you to know, however, that GLASS persuaded the local authorities to charge you no port dues and to make only nominal charges for repairs and replenishments."

"I suppose we should be grateful."

"You most certainly should be," Smith said definitely. He got to his feet. "Thank you for your hospitality. But I must go now. They are expecting me at the Iralian Embassy." As he shook hands with Trafford and the others he said, "You will be here for at least two more weeks. You will be hearing from us before you are ready for space."

When he was gone, Irene remarked, "So that's that. We haven't come out of it too badly. Even so, I shall see to it that the next charter, especially if it involves pulling other people's irons out of the fire, is much more advantageous to us."

"It might be even more advantageous," muttered Tallentire moodily, "to turn honest pirate. At least we should know where we stood."

"Pipe down, Second Mate," Irene told him.